Rugrats in Paris: THE MOVIE

Adapted by Cathy East Dubowski
and Mark Dubowski

Based on the Script by
David N. Weiss & J. David Stem
and
Jill Gorey & Barbara Herndon
and
Kate Boutilier

POCKET
BOOKS

Based on the TV series *Rugrats*® created by Klasky/Csupo Inc.
and Paul Germain as seen on BBC tv

POCKET
B O O K S

First published in Great Britain in 2001 by Simon & Schuster UK Ltd
Africa House, 64-78 Kingsway, London WC2B 6AH
Copyright © 1999 Viacom International Inc.

All rights reserved. NICKELODEON, *Rugrats,* and all related titles, logos, and
characters are trademarks of Viacom International Inc.

All rights reserved including the right of reproduction in whole or in part in any form.

POCKET BOOKS and colophon are registered trademarks
of Simon & Schuster.

A CIP catalogue for this book is available from the British Library

Printed and bound by Cox & Wyman Ltd, Reading, Berkshire

ISBN 0-743-41491-8

1 3 5 7 9 10 8 6 4 2

Chapter 1

Tommy Pickles tried not to squirm.

He was used to running around in nothing but a comfortable squishy nappy and a tiny blue T-shirt. Today his mummy had covered that up with a fancy tuxedo and a snug bow tie – party clothes.

But this was no party for Tommy. The room was dark and hushed. He had a problem and he had come to see somebody important – the one they called the Bobfather.

'I believe in the playground,' Tommy began, in a quiet voice. 'It's my favouritest place in the whole wild world. But two yesterdays ago a *bad* thing happened when we was playin' there.'

Tommy glanced down at his baby brother, Dil. For once Dil sat quietly in his pushchair, even though he, too, wore a scratchy tuxedo and tie.

3

Tommy sighed. Ever since Dil had been born, Tommy had had the responsibility of taking care of him. Now something really bad had happened to Dil. Tommy had to make it right. 'Some big boys tooked my brother's Binky,' he said, 'and buried it in the sandpit.'

'Binky bye-bye,' Dil piped up.

'They maked my brother cry,' Tommy said. 'So I said to Dilly, this is a job . . . for the Bobfather.'

Tommy's cousin, Angelica Pickles, nodded slowly from where she sat in a big leather chair and stroked her cat, Fluffy, who sat in her lap. After a moment of thought, she chomped on a big biscuit, then mumbled with her mouth full, 'You come to me, on the day of this wedding, and ask me to take care of the boys who made your brother cry?'

Tommy frowned at Angelica, the Bobfather. 'Uh, no. Dil just wants a new Binky.'

Angelica scowled. 'That's it?' she cried. 'A Binky? I don't get to squeeze no one's head? Or pull no one's hair?'

Tommy shrugged. 'Uh . . . no.'

 4

Dil gazed up and begged, 'Binky peeze?'

Angelica rolled her eyes. 'Dumb baby! Can't even make a good wish!' She should have known better than to play her new game with anyone under three. She'd had the idea from a movie on TV the night before. It was a movie for grown-ups, and her mum had dragged her away from it just when it started getting interesting.

But Angelica had seen enough to know it was all about this 'family'. The boss of the family was this old fat guy named the Bobfather. He sat in a big chair in a dark room. Everybody came to him with their problems. Then, if the Bobfather felt like it, he granted their wishes. Sort of like the Lizard of Oz, Angelica thought.

Angelica loved to boss the babies around. So she made up this new game. And of course she got to be the boss – the Bobfather.

'All right,' Angelica said with a sigh. She held out her hand like the Bobfather in the movie and ordered Dil, 'Kiss my ring.'

Dil gave the ring a slobbery kiss.

Angelica winced. 'Ewee! Go send the next one in! And tell 'em to bring a napkin!'

Tommy blinked. He didn't see a new Binky anywhere. He sighed and pushed Dil's pushchair out of the door. Maybe Angelica the Bobfather would do like grown-ups did. Maybe she'd make the wish come true 'in a minute'.

Tommy steered the pushchair through a crowd of big people. They were dancing and laughing and having a good time. The party was to celebrate a new bride and groom – Grandpa Lou and his new wife, Lulu. Tommy pushed Dil into the back garden, where the sounds from the house were faint. Nobody seemed to notice them.

Nobody seemed to notice what was happening to the wedding cake, either.

Tommy's friends, the twins Phil and Lil DeVille, were climbing up a teetering pile of presents to reach the wedding cake. It was a towering white cake with two little dolls on top. A daddy doll in a black suit like Tommy's. A mummy doll in a white dress and veil.

'Faster, Philip!' Lil shoved her brother. 'We gots to get to the peoples on the top!'

'I got dibs on the feets!' Phil said. He knew they would be crusted with icing.

6

Tommy stopped Dil's pushchair in front of the cake. 'Phil! Lil!' he called out. 'The Bobfather wants to see you – now.'

Phil and Lil froze. The Bobfather! They knew it had to be important. They could tell that much from Tommy's voice. The cake would have to wait.

Phil and Lil dragged a broken toy hobby-horse into the Bobfather's meeting room and held it up before Angelica. Lil shivered. Even Phil gulped. Angelica usually looked kind of mean and scary. As the Bobfather, she was meaner and scarier!

'Uh, Bobfather,' Phil said nervously. 'We founded this broken horse in our crib.'

'Well,' Angelica said, 'that's what you get for wiping your bogies on Cynthia.' Cynthia was Angelica's favourite doll.

Phil nodded and said, 'So that's where I left them.'

Meanwhile, on the dance floor, Chuckie Finster was dancing with Tommy's neighbour

7

Susie Carmichael. Chuckie was dressed up in a suit and bow tie. Susie had ribbons in her pigtails that matched her fancy dress.

Susie was a good dancer, but Chuckie wasn't. He stared at his feet while trying not to step on Susie's toes. 'Nine-eleven . . . twenty . . .'

'Chuckie!' Susie said. 'You're not supposed to look at your feet when you're dancing!'

'But I gots to, Susie!' Chuckie replied. 'They keep gettin' all tanglied up.'

At last the song ended. Chuckie heaved a sigh of relief.

'Ladies and gentlemen,' the man playing the record machine said into his microphone, 'let's give a warm round of applause to our number one newlyweds out of this week's top-ten married couples . . . Mr and Mrs Lou and Lulu Pickles!'

The wedding guests moved to the edges of the room. Grandpa Lou stepped to the centre of the dance floor with Lulu on his arm. The DJ began to play some swing music – music that was popular when Grandpa Lou was a young man.

'C'mon, Lulu!' Grandpa exclaimed. 'Let's show these whippersnappers how it's done!'

'I didn't get these plastic hips for nothin'!' Lulu replied.

Then the newlyweds began to dance. The wedding guests watched and smiled.

It's so sweet to see him happy again, Didi thought. Grandpa Lou had lost his first wife long, long ago. His hair was white and his hearing wasn't what it used to be. But when he danced with Lulu, he looked like a young man in love.

Didi glanced at her neighbour Chas Finster, Chuckie's dad. His beautiful wife, Melinda, had died when Chuckie was just a tiny baby. What a sad time that had been. Ever since then, Chas had been both father and mother to his son. And he had done a wonderful job.

But on a day like today, Didi couldn't help but wonder: Will Chas ever fall in love again? Will he ever think about getting married?

But no – I can't ask him, Didi thought. I wouldn't want to embarrass him –

'So, Chas, buddy,' Betty DeVille bellowed as

she slapped him on the back. 'Think you'll ever tie the knot again? 'Cause I got a cousin who's looking. Big bones, broad shoulders. And she can eat her weight in cheese in a single sitting.'

Didi didn't know whether to laugh or blush. Betty, Phil and Lil's mum, was a wonderful friend. But she did have a way of coming right out and saying things no one else dared to!

Chas was a shy kind of guy. A neat dresser, with his red hair, moustache and glasses, he was nice-looking in a quiet sort of way.

Betty's question seemed to embarrass him a little. 'Thanks, Betty, but cheese doesn't agree with me. Neither does dating.' He fiddled with his bow tie. 'Besides,' he added, 'Chuckie and I are very happy with the way things are.'

Chuckie opened the meeting-room door and looked inside for the Bobfather. The room was dark and spooky. Angelica perched on a big chair stroking her cat, Fluffy. With a sigh, he stepped inside. Fluffy purred.

Chuckie didn't know if he should speak first

or wait for Angelica – the Bobfather – to begin. So he waited. He pushed his glasses up on his nose. He fiddled with his fancy bow tie.

'You're like family to me, Finster,' Angelica said. 'Name your wish.'

'Um, uh . . . gosh, Bobfather!' Chuckie stuttered. 'I don't know what to wish for.'

'Just pick something already!' Angelica yelled impatiently.

Chuckie picked his nose and thought.

'I don't mean your nose!' Angelica shouted.

Chuckie took a step back. He didn't want to make Angelica mad, but he hadn't had enough time.

The door swung open. Susie Carmichael poked her head in. 'C'mon, Chuckie! Grandpa Lou is throwing the gardener!' She meant, 'garter'. It was an old tradition to throw one to the crowd at a wedding. Whoever caught it was supposed to have good luck.

Chuckie wasn't sure what that was all about. But he figured it must be more fun than getting yelled at by Angelica. So he let Susie drag him from the room.

11

Angelica sat up on the edge of her chair. How dare Chuckie Finster leave before she had finished the game! She marched out after him. Angelica scowled as she searched the crowd. Where were those dumb babies, anyway?

There they were – huddled on the side of the dance floor. Angelica stomped over. On her way she passed a pushchair with a tiny baby sucking happily on a dummy. Without a second thought, Angelica snatched it out of the baby's mouth. 'I'll take that Binky!'

'Waaaah!'

'Shh!' Angelica snapped. She crossed the room and popped the wet dummy straight into Dil's mouth. 'Here ya go, drooly! Fell off a truck!'

Tommy's eyes lit up. Chuckie gasped. Phil and Lil clapped, they were so impressed.

A new dummy! Just what Tommy had asked for. The Bobfather was *amazing*! Like magic, she had made Dil's wish come true.

More than ever, Chuckie knew he had to be careful what he wished for.

Chapter 2

Grandpa Lou couldn't remember when he'd had more fun. Taking a break from the dancing, he helped himself to some sparkling pink punch set out on the refreshment table.

'I'm really happy for you, Pop,' Drew said, slapping Grandpa Lou on the back.

'Yeah,' Stu said, 'Lulu's a great lady.'

'Yep,' Lou agreed, 'she's a keeper.' Then a tear glistened in one eye. ''Course, no one'll ever replace your mother,' he said. He tapped his chest above his heart. 'Fact is, it's her love in here that helped this ol' geezer love again.'

'All right, folks!' the DJ shouted. 'It's time for a special dance for all the kids and their mums.' Excited chatter rippled across the room. Mums and kids of all ages spilled on to the dance floor.

Tommy and Dil giggled as Didi scooped them into her arms. 'Can Mummy have this dance?' she asked.

Betty hauled Phil and Lil into the air and sat one on each hip. Dr Lucy Carmichael twirled her little girl, Susie, across the floor. Charlotte even put down her cell phone long enough to call for her darling Angelica. Every child had a mother to dance with.

Every child except Chuckie. Chuckie was kind of used to being left out when it came to mummies. Most of the time, his daddy was almost as good . . . A lump rose in his throat.

But sometimes he couldn't help it. Sometimes he wished . . . Chuckie's face lit up.

That's it!

He broke out into a grin as Angelica ran past to dance with her mother.

'Angelica!' Chuckie shouted happily. 'I think I know what to wish for now!'

Chapter 3

Angelica stopped with her hands on her hips. She glared at Chuckie impatiently.

Softly, almost afraid to ask, Chuckie said, 'I'd kind of like to have a new mummy.'

Angelica shrugged. 'I'm tired of playing that game. 'Sides, I'm wanted on the dance floor!' She ran into Charlotte's arms.

Chuckie sighed. He watched Angelica and all the other children dance with their mummies. 'But that's my wish,' he whispered, even though he knew no one was there to hear.

Across the floor Chas sat alone. He thought about his late wife, Melinda, and wished she could be there to dance with Chuckie.

Hmm, all of the other kids were dancing. Where was Chuckie?

Chas spotted him, all alone, watching the

15

other children and swaying to the music. Chas's heart ached. He walked over and laid a hand on Chuckie's shoulder. Chas wished he could say something that would make the sadness go away. But all he could think of to say was, 'It's getting late, Chuckie. What do you say we head home?'

Chuckie raised his arms. Chas picked him up and carried his little boy home.

Back home Chas tucked Chuckie into bed and kissed him good night. Then he went to his own room and changed into his pyjamas. As he hung up his tuxedo in his closet, he noticed a box on a shelf.

A very special box.

He opened the box and began to look at the treasures inside. A journal written in a lady's lovely handwriting. A few garden tools. Photos. A raggedy teddy bear.

They were just things. Ordinary things. But they were things that had been a part of his wife's life. The things were still here, but she had gone.

The bedroom door creaked and a sleepy-looking Chuckie toddled in.

'What are you doing up?' Chas asked.

Chuckie looked at the things spread out on the bedspread. They were strange things, yet somehow . . . familiar.

And that bear. He couldn't take his eyes off that bear . . .

Chas smiled. 'I was just looking through some of our old things.' He held up the raggedy old bear. 'Do you remember your Wawa?'

Chuckie's face lit up. He threw his arms around the bear and hugged him tight.

Chas laughed softly. 'I guess you do!' He searched in the box and pulled out a photograph. He held it up for Chuckie to see. In the picture Chas and Melinda held baby Chuckie. Baby Chuckie was holding Wawa the bear.

Chuckie curled up next to Chas and hugged Wawa tight. He liked to listen to the sound of his daddy's voice. It made him feel happy, and safe, and – *yawn!* – sleepy . . .

'Ah, Chuckie,' Chas said. 'Your mum was an amazing woman. I'll bet your mum's in heaven

looking down on us. Oh, I miss her so much, Chuckie.' He sighed and watched Chuckie's eyes drift closed.

'You know,' he said, 'we could use a mummy's touch around here, couldn't we, little guy?'

But Chuckie didn't hear his father's words. He was too busy dreaming about the new mummy he was wishing for.

Chapter 4

'What are they doin', Tommy?' Chuckie whispered the next day. He and his friends were in Tommy's back garden, peeking through the basement window. That's where Tommy's daddy worked, making weird and wonderful things, like Dactar, the flying pterodactyl that shot real fire, or the amazing Reptar Wagon. Now Stu and Chas were hunched over the computer that sat among Stu's half-finished inventions on his work-table.

Tommy held up Dil so he could see too. Chuckie held up Wawa the bear.

'My daddy's helping your daddy catch some dates in a net,' Tommy whispered back.

'What are dates?' Chuckie asked.

'Big raisins that make you poo,' Phil explained.

19

The others nodded.

'What is it with you babies and poo?' Angelica fumed.

'Gosh,' Tommy said. 'Where do you want us to start?'

Down in the basement Stu said, 'You gotta love the Internet, Chas. Behold the future of dating.'

'Wow!' Chas breathed. He shoved his glasses up on his nose and peered at the screen. 'My own web page!' The headline read:

CHAS FINSTER – BUREAUCRAT/BACHELOR.

Beneath that, a colour picture of him filled the screen. All anyone had to do was point and click to find out all kinds of things about him: his height, his weight, his underwear size, his hobbies . . .

'Are you sure this is going to work?' he asked Stu.

Stu chuckled. Chas wasn't the only guy out there who wanted a date, right? He had to stand out from the crowd. He had to advertise.

'Would I do you wrong?' he replied. 'Look, you already have twelve dates!'

'That's triple my lifetime record,' Chas said in amazement.

Stu double-clicked with the mouse and a dozen photos appeared on the screen. Photos of prospective dates.

'Look at this one!' Chas exclaimed. 'She loves sunsets, long walks on sandy beaches, and is not allowed in the state of Kentucky.'

Chas sighed and said, 'Oh, I don't know about this, Stu!'

Out in the back garden the babies were puzzled. What were the daddies doing?

'Let me put it to you this way,' Angelica said with a sigh. 'Dates is for people like Mr Chuckie's dad who don't got no wife.'

'But why does Chuckie's daddy need a wife?' Lil asked.

'Ahh! What I have to put up with!' Angelica complained. ''Cause if his daddy gets a new wife, then that means Chuckie gets a new mummy.'

All the babies gasped.

Chuckie could hardly believe it. 'I'm really going to get my wish?' he breathed.

'Yup.' Angelica glanced around at all the amazed faces. She took a moment to enjoy being the centre of attention. Hey, Chuckie's gonna get a new mummy, right? she thought. I might as well take the credit! These dumb babies will never know the difference.

'Yeah,' she said. 'So long as you stay in my good flavour.'

'I didn't know she had a good flavour,' Lil whispered to Phil.

'Guys! Guys!' Chuckie cried. 'I'm gonna gets a new mummy! I bet she's gonna be clean and cuddly and nice.'

Chapter 5

Halfway around the world the sun shone on a peaceful Japanese village. Birds sang. Children ran and played.

Suddenly the ground shook. *Boom! Boom!*

A horrible roar split the air. *Rowwwrrr!*

A huge blast of fire shot down from the sky. A monster was coming. A giant Tyrannosaurus rex – Reptar!

The mighty Reptar threw back its scaly green head to roar – *Thunk!*

And its scaly green head fell off. It bounced and rolled to a stop just a few inches from the nose of a very angry-looking Frenchwoman.

This wasn't a Japanese village at all. It was a pretend village set up on a huge stage. The village people were all actors in a show at Reptarland, the newest theme park in Paris,

France. It was built by Yamaguchi Industries, a Japanese toy company.

The giant Reptar? It was only a mechanical dinosaur whose head kept falling off!

The Frenchwoman – Coco LaBouche – was in charge of all of Reptarland. She looked like an elegant Paris model – and had the personality of a fire-breathing dragon in a very bad mood. All the actors and stage workers froze when the Reptar head stopped in front of her.

Madame LaBouche was *not* happy. And when Madame wasn't happy – somebody was in *big* trouble.

Coco's assistant, a sweet-looking Japanese woman named Kira, kept her head bowed over her notepad. She held her pencil, ready to write any notes Madame wanted to dictate. She held her breath, waiting to see what Madame would say or do.

Coco's face turned red with rage. She glared at Jean-Claude, her right-hand man. 'Jean-Claude,' she said through clenched teeth, 'tell me what *buffoon* is responsible for this head-challenged amphibian!'

Jean-Claude's nose wrinkled in disgust. 'It's that gauche toy designer named Cucumber – *non*! Tomato! *Non . . .* Pickles! Stewed Pickles!'

'Ah, *oui*. I want that American in Paris within twenty-four hours,' Coco ordered. 'Or *another* head will roll!'

Jean-Claude nodded crisply. 'I'll take care of it – *personally*.'

Coco grunted and marched up to the stage.

Kira let out a huge breath and relaxed – just a little. For now, at least, Madame LaBouche's anger was aimed at a different target.

'This is a disgrace!' Coco screamed at her employees as she paced the stage. 'I seem to have employed nothing but amateurs! *Non*, worse than amateurs – you're *dabblers*! I have a good mind to send you all back to the croissant carts and hire real professionals!' She paused to catch her breath and kick the huge Reptar head with the pointed toe of her stylish French shoe. 'I want the head of this decapitated creature in my office *tout de suite*! And don't make a mess on my carpets! *Comprenez-vous?*'

Jean-Claude turned to Kira. He had told

25

Madame that he would take care of the Pickles problem personally. And he would – by personally ordering someone else to do it. 'Kira,' he said, 'Madame wants her Pickles. Now.'

Ring! Ring! Ring!

Halfway around the world, in a small town in America, it was the middle of the night. Stu Pickles snored as he dreamed. He was dreaming about a new invention . . .

Ring! Ring! Ring!

Don't tell me I invented the telephone, Stu thought. Still half asleep, he reached out and felt around on his bedside table. He picked up the phone receiver and brought it to his ear. 'Hello?' he mumbled.

'Hello, Mr Pickles?' said a woman with a slight Japanese accent. 'This is Kira Watanabe from Reptarland. I'm sorry to call so late . . .'

Stu snored into the phone.

'Mr Pickles! The Reptar that you designed has broken down and my boss is having a fit.'

'Reptar's a hit?' Stu said sleepily. 'That's

great . . .' While still holding the receiver, he burrowed beneath his pillow and began to snore again.

'Mr Pickles!' Kira said urgently. 'We need you to come to Paris on the next flight.'

'Paris?' Stu mumbled. 'Oh, yeah, the City of Light . . .'

'Madame kindly recommends that – '

'Come with family and friends?' Stu asked. 'Okey-dokey.'

Yawning, Stu hung up the phone and plopped face-down on the bed. 'Hey, Deed,' he mumbled into his pillow. 'We're going to France . . .'

Didi snuggled deeper into the covers. 'No, Stu,' she said, 'I'm too tired to dance . . .'

Stu and Didi began to drift back to sleep.

All was still.

Suddenly they sat bolt upright in bed. They stared at each other with wide-open eyes. 'France?' they both exclaimed.

Chapter 6

Now that Stu Pickles, his family and some of their close friends were going to Paris, France, there was so much to do to get ready!

First, Angelica had to find someone to brag to. She made her mum dial up Susie Carmichael, who wasn't going on the trip with them. 'I'm going to France and you're not and I already learned how to *parsley-voo francy* – which for *your* information means "speak French".' She smiled and waited for Susie to admire her.

Maybe Susie wasn't going to France, but she did happen to be studying French in her nursery school. To Angelica, she replied, '*Mais j'ai mal aux oreilles pour les français qui vont t'entendre. Au revoir!*'

She knew Angelica would have no idea she had just said, 'My ears hurt for the French

people who will hear you. Goodbye!'

Angelica stared blankly at the phone. 'No one likes a show-off, Susie.'

Then everyone had to have their pictures taken for passports. Chuckie had his picture taken with Wawa.

Then there was the packing. Chas packed a suitcase just for his allergy medications, inhalers, tissues and a humidifier. All Chuckie cared about taking was Wawa. Betty and Howard had to pack two of everything for the twins. Stu packed Spike into a portable kennel. He was going too.

Before they knew it, they were on the plane and ready for take-off. The engines roared and the plane started to move down the runway. Then the wheels left the ground. The babies looked out of their windows in delight as the houses, trees and cars grew smaller.

Didi played 'This little piggy . . .' with Dil's toes. Nearby, Chuckie watched them, then looked down at his own toes. He wiggled them,

wishing he had a mummy to play with them too.

Most of the grown-ups were twisted around in their seats, trying to sleep. The flight to Paris would take many hours. But the babies were too excited to sleep. The aeroplane was like a big playground in the sky to them. Phil and Tommy brought out their Reptar and Robosnail toys to play with.

'I am Reptar!' Tommy said in a growly voice. 'Hear me roar!'

Robosnail went flying into the aisle.

'Oops!' Phil said. 'Guess Robosnail thought he could fly.'

'Poor Robosnail,' Lil said.

As the babies looked at Robosnail, they noticed a little boy across the aisle pushing a button on the arm of his chair. A light flashed above his head in the shape of a woman. Chuckie wondered if it was some kind of game. But a moment later a motherly-looking flight attendant hurried to the boy's side. She was pretty and smelled nice and smiled at the boy as she handed him a blanket.

'Look at that, you guys!' Tommy exclaimed.

30

'I never saw a mummy button before,' Chuckie said.

Two seats back they spotted a baby girl sitting on her father's lap. She reached over to the chair arm, trying to press the same kind of button. As soon as her fingertips touched it, her mummy came and sat down. She smiled at the girl and began to read to her from a book.

Chuckie was awestruck. Nobody told him you could get mummies on an aeroplane. He looked at his friends in amazement.

'Let's see what kind of mummy your button gots for you, Chuckie,' Lil suggested eagerly. *Smack!* She gave Chuckie's mummy button an extra-strong whack.

'Hey, I wanted to press the button, Lillian!' Phil complained.

'You want the button, Philip?' Lil asked. She shook her head. 'You can't handle the button.'

As the twins argued, Chuckie waited anxiously to see what kind of mummy would come. Seconds later a tall, surly flight attendant tramped down the aisle. She stomped on Phil's plastic Robosnail.

Crunch!

She raised her shoe and said, 'Oh, look. A toy that was already broken. Unfortunately, the union forbids me from picking it up. That's a job for your mummy.'

Chuckie cowered in his seat as she stared at him, then sighed in relief as she walked off in a huff.

'Somebody got up on the wrong side of the bread,' Phil muttered.

Lil reached for the button. 'Let's try again – '

'No!' Chuckie said in a terrified voice. 'Let's not, Lil. I'll just wait for the Bobfather to bring her. Whenever that is.'

Tommy noticed Angelica sneaking down the aisle towards the front of the plane. He watched as she disappeared behind a curtain. 'Let's go ask her. She just sneaked behind that curtain.'

Together they toddled up the aisle and through the curtain. It was the first-class section, but the babies didn't know that. They found Angelica sitting in a seat listening to music with headphones. She hummed and kicked the seat in front of her. With each kick

the seat lurched forward and back. The man who was sitting in front of her grabbed his airsickness bag.

Tommy unplugged Angelica's headphones. She sat up in surprise. 'Hey! What's the big idea?'

'Hi, Angelica!' Chuckie said cheerfully.

Angelica frowned when she saw them. 'Oh, for feet's sake.' She waved her hand at the other passengers. They were all grown-ups. Most were men wearing business suits. 'Can't you see this is the "no dumb babies" section?'

'Sorry, Angelica,' Tommy said. 'But Chuckie was wonderin' when his new mummy was comin'.'

Angelica bit her lip. She'd forgotten all about Chuckie and his dumb wish. 'I'm, um, working on it. But I got so hungry I had to sit down.'

'Maybe you need a nap,' Chuckie suggested.

'Or biscuits,' Angelica muttered.

Chuckie nodded. 'Or biscuits.'

Angelica grinned as an idea formed in her head. 'And ice cream.'

'And ice cream!' Chuckie agreed.

33

'Which happens to be in that kitchen up there.' Angelica pointed.

Chuckie wanted to keep Angelica happy while she was working on his important wish. 'Be right back,' he told her. 'Come on, guys.'

He and Tommy marched towards the kitchen. Angelica put her headphones back on. Phil and Lil were happy crawling under the seats.

'Where are they going?' Lil wondered. 'There's lots of neat stuffs down here, Philip. Like a hairy toofbrush, a 'tato chip – '

Phil found an airsickness bag and looked inside. 'Hey, somebody musta losted their lunch.'

Lil peeked over his shoulder. 'Mmmm.'

Meanwhile Chuckie and Tommy had reached the plane's small kitchen. They spotted biscuits up high, but some shiny carts were in their way. Chuckie was determined to take something back to Angelica. So he pulled out a cart to climb on.

Just then the plane tilted as it banked to one side among the fluffy clouds.

'Uh-oh!' Chuckie squeaked. He'd just learned

34

something special about the shiny carts.

They didn't have the brakes on!

'Tommyyyy!'

Tommy watched wide-eyed as his friend began to roll down the aisle of the plane. It picked up speed, rolled past a startled flight attendant (the mean one who had crushed Phil's toy) and crashed into a control panel. All the oxygen masks over each passenger's seat dropped down, dangling by tiny plastic hoses. Chuckie flew off the cart and landed in Angelica's lap.

'*Finster!*' Angelica hollered.

Phil and Lil pulled down a couple of oxygen masks. 'Look, Philip,' Lil exclaimed in delight. 'Party hats!'

If the flight attendant had been mean before, she was a snarling grizzly bear by now. She quickly herded the babies out of first class.

'Thanks a lot, nappy-bags!' Angelica yelled at the babies.

'Note to self,' the surly flight attendant muttered. 'At the next union meeting, demand that children ride with the baggage.'

The babies ran and jumped on to their mummies' laps. Except for Chuckie. He crawled back into his seat.

'Whew!' Betty said with a hearty laugh. 'I smell a pair of pooey pups!'

'Come on, sweetie,' Didi said to Tommy. 'Time to get changed.'

The two women headed up the aisle to the rest room to change their children. Chuckie smiled up at his daddy, who had fallen asleep. Then he looked out of the window.

The sun shone behind the clouds, making them glow. Chuckie marvelled at the shapes he saw floating by the window: a teddy bear, Reptar the dinosaur, a baby bottle, a frog. Then . . . a cloud that took the shape of his mother's face.

Chuckie gasped. 'Mummy . . .'

He wanted to talk to the Mummy cloud. Even though I can't talk grown-up talk yet, he thought, she'll understand, anyway. She's my mummy. He wanted to talk to her about his search for a new mummy. He wanted a mum who would hold him when he cried. Who

36

would hold his hand when he crossed the road. Who would chase the monsters away and play with him when he was lonely. He held up Wawa for the Mummy cloud to see.

But then the wind began to blow the clouds into different shapes. Fat, fluffy chunks drifted off the dinosaur and turned into bunnies. The frog turned into a shoe. The smiling Mummy cloud faded into wisps of cloud. Cloud wisps that looked like nothing. Nothing at all.

A tear rolled down Chuckie's cheek. He knew what kind of mum he really wanted. A mum who would stay for ever. A mum who would *never* say goodbye.

Chapter 7

The babies slept peacefully all night on the plane. About mid-morning they began to feel strange. At first Chuckie thought the plane was falling! He clutched Wawa with one hand and grabbed his daddy with the other. Soon – with a little bump – the plane landed on a long driveway. Chuckie looked out of the window. Paris, France, looked a lot like the airport back home.

The plane taxied to a stop. A trailer drove up and men began to unload the luggage from the belly of the plane. The grown-ups got ready to leave the plane.

After getting off the plane, the babies and their parents had to have their passports checked. A man in a uniform looked at their pictures and used a big stamp to stamp each booklet.

Then they all went on a long escalator to a

big room. It had a round moving counter like a merry-go-round in the middle of the room. It was a special merry-go-round just for suitcases!

All of the suitcases came out of a large hole in the wall and rode on the merry-go-round. The families collected their bags and headed to the airport exit. Cars and taxis clogged the street. A man dressed in a Reptar suit held up a sign that said PICKLES. 'Welcome to Paris,' he greeted them. 'I've been asked to take you directly to Reptarland.' He led the families to a Reptarland bus.

'Outta my way, babies!' Angelica shouted, shoving her way through. 'The prettiest, smartest, bestest girl gets the front seat!'

'So why is *she* in such a hurry?' Phil asked.

The bus went on to the motorway headed for town. The babies waved bye-bye to the aeroplane. When they drove further into Paris, the streets became twisty and turny.

'Uhh, my tummy's all bubbly,' Lil moaned.

'Don't worry, Lil,' Phil said. 'I've got your Baggie from the plane.'

The babies spotted their destination before

39

their parents did. 'Wow!' they all shouted. 'Reptarland!'

It looked as big as a whole town! It was noisy with the sound of roller-coasters. It smelled like candyfloss! The babies looked around in awe. This was the bestest place in the world!

The bus drove through the huge entrance gates and stopped in front of a large fancy hotel. People poured off the bus.

'I've been waiting my entire whole life to see this!' Phil exclaimed.

'Look!' Chuckie exclaimed. 'Reptar's house! We must be in Pokyo!'

'Pokyo?' Angelica said. 'Don't you know nothin'? We're in Parrots!'

The babies stared blankly at her.

'Parrots?' Angelica repeated. 'City of Lice? Home of Napoley-ish Blownapart?' She sighed and shook her head in disgust. 'What's the use? You're just as dumb here as you are at home.'

'Welcome to Reptarland,' the bus driver announced.

'Yay!' the babies cheered.

The families crowded into the hotel foyer and went in the fancy lifts up to their rooms.

'*Voilà!*' Stu said as he opened the door to their suite. 'Our Parisian pied-à-terre!'

'Boy,' Betty said, looking around. 'Pretty posh digs. Whoa! This jar of nuts costs more than Howard's hair implants!' She gobbled them down in one gulp.

Howard relaxed on the bed. 'The beds are quite comfortable,' he said.

'Yeah?' said Betty. 'Incoming!' She flopped down on the bed with a force that sent Howard flying. He crash-landed on the floor.

'And so's the floor,' Howard added.

Just then Angelica stormed in. 'Hey!' she cried. 'Which one of you babies put your pooey nappy in my suitcase?'

Phil looked around, whistling nonchalantly.

In the next room Charlotte and Drew had already dumped their bags and were ready to explore Paris. 'We're off to the boutiques!' Charlotte called. 'Would you keep an eye on Angelica? Wonderful!' she said, without waiting for an answer. '*Au revoir!*'

'Okay,' Stu said, 'it's time to meet Ms LaBouche – the woman who made all this possible. Shall we?'

But jet lag had caught up with Betty, Howard, Didi and even Spike. They were all sound asleep.

'Well,' Stu said to Chas, 'looks like it's you and me and the kids. Are you ready?'

'*Oui, oui, mon ami*,' Chas replied.

They left with the babies toddling behind them. Chuckie, the last one out, slammed the door. Inside the room, the noise woke up Spike. He went to the door and scratched. When a maid peeked in the room, Spike slipped out between her legs. By the time he reached the lift, the doors had closed. He sniffed along the hallway until he found a door with fresh air – the stairwell. For a dog, stairs were faster than lifts, anyway. In a few minutes he was exploring the street.

A short time later, in a high-rise office building, another lift door opened and out stepped Stu,

Chas, Angelica and the babies.

A pretty Japanese lady approached them and smiled. '*Bonjour!* Welcome to Reptarland. One of you must be Mr Pickles.'

'That would be *moi*,' Stu replied. He hoped she noticed how easily he dropped the French word for 'me' into the conversation. It was one of the French words he'd learned on the plane. 'And this is my friend, Charles Finster.'

The grown-ups shook hands. Chuckie was so busy looking around, he dropped his bear. The Japanese woman picked it up, handed it to him, and gave him a warm smile.

'This is my son, Chuckie,' Chas said.

'Hi, Chuckie! I'm Kira. Oh, I like your bear!'

Chuckie gave her a huge smile. Some grown-ups were too busy to notice bears.

Then Kira smiled at the babies. 'What sweet children! Is this your first time in Paris?'

'France, yes,' Chas replied. 'But I've been to Paris, Texas, a number of times. I like the two-stepping festivals. That little dance is really quite invigorating. Do you know it?'

'I'm afraid not,' Kira said.

Yack, yack, yack! Angelica hated it when the grown-ups started talking and forgot about her! She looked around a partly open door marked COCO LABOUCHE. This was the woman Stu Pickles had come to see. But Angelica couldn't read. She simply ducked inside.

Coco LaBouche sat at a huge fancy desk. Beside the desk stood a gleaming table. And on the table was a *giant* fancy sweet dish full of chocolates!

Coco was scowling at something on her desk. Behind her, Jean-Claude stood with his back to the room as he stared out of the window at Reptarland.

Angelica grinned. She was an expert at sneaking into rooms without being seen – especially if the room contained chocolate! She grabbed the bowl and dived beneath the desk to hide with her loot.

Phil and Lil had followed her. They were awestruck at the sight of Reptar's mechanical head sitting in the middle of the floor.

'I bet the Bobfather had something to do with this,' Phil whispered to Lil.

 44

But Coco LaBouche still hadn't noticed the children. She was too busy staring out of the window at the crowds in the theme park below.

'Thousands of children laughing, skipping, frolicking,' she said. 'They *disgust* me.'

Suddenly she turned around and spotted Phil and Lil as they crawled across the floor. 'Jean-Claude!' she shrieked. 'Where did those *filthy* little bookends come from?'

The bookends – Phil and Lil DeVille – froze. Then Tommy and Chuckie crawled into view.

'They're multiplying!' Coco gasped. 'Jean-Claude! Call the dog-catcher! The caretaker! Do something!'

'*Oui*, Madame.' Jean-Claude went to the door and did what he always did when there was something to be done. He told somebody else to do it. 'Kira!'

Kira hurried in. She gasped when she saw the babies crawling around the office and quickly rounded them up by the door. 'Come along, children. Um, Madame, Mr Pickles is here.'

'Oh, good,' Coco replied. 'Send in the clown.'

45

Oh, dear! Kira crossed her fingers for Mr Pickles and led the babies outside.

Coco settled back into her chair, waiting with glittering eyes.

Stu eagerly entered the room. He thought he was here to be praised for his wonderful work on the giant Reptar. He stood before Madame LaBouche's desk and waited for the compliments to flow.

'So,' Coco drawled sarcastically, 'if it isn't our brilliant designer . . .'

Stu blushed. 'Well, I wouldn't say brilliant – '

'Neither would I.' Coco hit a button on her desk that automatically slammed the door.

Stu was confused. That's when he looked closer at the huge Reptar head sitting in the middle of the floor. It looked awfully familiar. Like the head on the Reptar *he* had built. *Gulp!*

Coco rose from her chair. '*Écoutez*, Monsieur Pickles! This high-tech slab of steel' – she pointed at the broken Reptar head – 'is an unforgivable *disaster*! I have never seen such ineptitude in my entire life!'

Stu winced and turned pale. This was not

the welcome he'd been expecting at all.

'The show had not even begun,' Coco shouted, 'and your precious "Reptar" had taken his first fall! I don't care if you have to work twenty-four hours a day! I want that giant tin can *fixed*! Do you hear me?'

Stu opened his mouth to explain.

Outside Madame LaBouche's office, in the reception area, Chas and Kira looked at each other over the babies' heads. They could hear every word Coco shouted, loud and clear.

Kira looked embarrassed. But then she suddenly brightened. 'Why don't we take the babies to see the Princess Parade while my boss and Mr Pickles . . .'

She cringed as another string of shouts came from Coco's office.

'. . . get better acquainted?' she finished.

'Oh! The kids would love that,' Chas was quick to agree. He and Kira quickly shooed the babies towards the lift. Tommy, Chuckie, Phil and Lil happily ran inside. In their haste, they didn't miss Angelica, whom they had left behind in Madame LaBouche's office. Just as

the doors of the lift closed, the door to Madame LaBouche's office banged open.

'See this face?' Madame screamed, pointing to her face. It was a terrifying mask of fury.

Stu flinched.

'I never want to make this face again!' Coco shouted. 'Now get to work!'

Stu backed towards the door. 'I'll have it working in no time,' he assured her. '"Mechanical expertise" is my middle name.'

'Then your first name should be "I have no,"' Madame LaBouche shot back.

Stu hurried out of the office so fast that he accidentally shut the door on his tie and choked. 'Ouch!' He freed himself, then dashed for the lift, feeling lucky to be alive.

Chapter 8

Once the Americans were gone, Coco LaBouche's phone rang.

Jean-Claude peered over his newspaper at it, but didn't move. Only Coco answered this special phone. 'It's the boss,' he pointed out.

Coco was *his* boss. But even Coco had a boss. The Big Boss. Mr Yamaguchi, the Japanese businessman who owned Reptarland.

Coco threw up her hands and strode towards the phone. 'As if I don't have enough to do! Bosses can be such a bother.'

Jean-Claude's eyebrow twitched. 'I hadn't noticed.'

Coco hit another button on her remote control. Instantly a whole wall of TV screens came to life, each one filled with the smiling face of Mr Yamaguchi. He looked like

someone's grandfather, with white hair, kind eyes and a gentle smile. Coco instantly twisted her scowl into a smile. 'Monsieur Yamaguchi! So nice to see you.'

Mr Yamaguchi bowed his head slightly. 'As you know, I'm stepping down as president of Yamaguchi Industries and I've begun a search for my replacement.'

'Splendid!' Coco exclaimed. 'I accept!'

Mr Yamaguchi politely ignored her poor manners and said simply, 'You are *one* of the many under consideration.'

'But I've made millions for this company!' Coco exclaimed in astonishment.

'The candidate should not be concerned only with money,' Mr. Yamaguchi explained patiently. 'He or she must understand what it means to bring joy to children. In fact, he or she must have the heart of a child.'

Coco nodded as if she agreed. But under her breath she muttered, 'I must have one in a jar somewhere.'

'Excuse me?' Mr. Yamaguchi said.

'I said, uh – my heart is ajar with love for

children! It's a French thing. I simply adore money – er, children. In fact, I'm engaged to a wonderful man with a baby thing all his own.'

Jean-Claude's eyebrows shot up at Coco's lie. Then he leaned against her desk and smiled to cover for her in front of Mr Yamaguchi.

Angelica reached for a chocolate and almost lost her hand as Coco's foot slammed on top of Jean-Claude's foot to warn him.

Mr Yamaguchi looked delighted at Coco's news. 'Congratulations, Madame! I look forward to attending the wedding and seeing you with your new family. We'll discuss the promotion then. Goodbye.'

Mr Yamaguchi clicked off. Coco stood staring at the blackened screen.

'What now, Pinocchio?' Jean-Claude asked.

Coco ran her hands through her hair. '*Years of clawing my way to the top – gone to waste! Why am I not some child's tender mother?*' She banged on the table in frustration. 'Why? Why? Why?' Beneath the desk, Angelica jumped each time Coco pounded the desk with her fist.

Jean-Claude glanced at his nails. 'I can't

imagine. I've always thought of you as a mother.'

Coco shot him a nasty look. Jean-Claude could be obnoxious, but he was as heartless as she was and just as ambitious. He carried out all her orders without a blink. Coco strode to the window and stared out across the crowds of Reptarland. 'There has to be a spineless little man with a brat of his own somewhere out there.'

Crash!

Coco whirled around. Jean-Claude jumped to his feet. They stared beneath the table. Angelica Pickles smiled back at them. Her face was smeared with chocolate. In her greediness, she had knocked over the bowl. 'Oops.'

Coco strode to the desk and bent over to tug the child out.

Once on her feet, Angelica smoothed out her dress and fluffed her two blonde pigtails. *'Bonbon?'* she said innocently.

'My expensive chocolates are in her little American stomach!' Coco exclaimed. 'Jean-Claude, get them back!'

'No, wait!' Angelica cried. When Coco slowly

turned around, Angelica held out her hand. One last piece of chocolate lay melting in her palm. She thrust it towards Coco.

Coco knocked the chocolate from Angelica's hand and grabbed her by the collar. 'You have five seconds to come up with a reason why I shouldn't lock you up for ever and ever.'

Angelica was usually good with excuses, but this lady was scary! 'Um . . . because I can stick five raisins up my nose, and I can sing real good, and for ever and ever is a really long time – '

'Tick tock,' Coco said, tapping her foot impatiently.

'And I know where you can find a spiny little man with a brat of his own!' Angelica blurted in desperation.

Coco halted in mid-shout. 'Jean-Claude,' she said. 'I think I've just made a friend.'

Chapter 9

'Wow!' Tommy said. 'I never seen anything like this afore! Isn't this neat, Chuckie?'

The Princess Parade filled the park's main street with colour and noise. Women in brightly coloured kimonos danced to the rhythm of 'The Princess Spectacular Song'. Samurai warriors imitated a fierce battle with their swords.

'I dunno, Tommy,' Chuckie said nervously. He watched the samurai warriors with their flashing swords. 'There's something weird about a guy in a ponytail and a dress.'

'I like the ponytail,' Lil said.

'I like the dress,' Phil said.

The babies looked at Phil.

'What?' he asked.

Chas and Kira stood with the children. But neither one of them was watching the parade.

They were watching each other. Chas was impressed with how nicely Kira had gathered the children and how gentle and sweet she was when she talked with them. 'Gee, Kira,' he said shyly. 'You're a natural.'

'Oh, well.' Kira blushed. 'I have a beautiful little girl to thank for that. Kimi's almost two.'

'So's my Chuckie!' Chas blurted out. 'Not a girl, I mean.' He blushed. 'But, you know.'

Chas and Kira turned back to the parade. A float glided past carrying a princess. She waved from a pagoda-like castle. Women in kimonos threw flower petals in its path.

'Look!' Kira said to the children. 'The princess is coming! Would you like me to tell you her story?'

The babies nodded and cooed. Kira smiled and began, 'Once upon a time, there was a mighty dinosaur named Reptar. Everyone ran away from him except the beautiful princess. She wasn't afraid, because she could see that Reptar wasn't vicious. He was lonely and unhappy. So she promised to take care of him and keep him safe and loved for ever and ever.'

Just then the float passed right in front of the children. The princess looked down at them with a lovely smile.

She's smiling at me! Chuckie thought.

As she waved her hand, the air sparkled. The sparkle was actually glitter. But Chuckie didn't know that. To him, it looked like magic. Chuckie smiled up through the glittering shower at the beautiful princess. He held out his hand to catch some of her magic. When he looked into the palm of his hand, it sparkled like a magic promise.

Chuckie pushed up his glasses and watched the princess float away with the parade. He was totally enchanted. 'For ever and ever . . .,' he murmured.

Across the park, in Coco LaBouche's office, magical sprinkles rained down for Angelica, too. Magical *sweetie* sprinkles – her favourite – pouring down on to a huge bowl of ice cream.

Wow, Angelica thought as she watched Jean-Claude dump more sprinkles on to the ice

cream. Her mummy and daddy gave her almost everything she wanted, but they *never* let her have *that* much!

Angelica stuffed a huge spoonful of the cold sweet treat into her mouth. She knew Madame LaBouche was only being nice to her so she would spill her guts about Mr Chuckie's Dad. But so what? It was worth it. She licked her spoon, then revealed, 'My mummy says Mr Chuckie's Dad is so desperate that he'll marry the first lady who plops the question.'

Coco's eyebrow arched. 'Excellent. Now, run along before you give me lice.'

Angelica frowned thoughtfully. She'd been getting her way with her mummy and daddy and uncles and aunts since she was still in the playpen. Maybe she wasn't milking this situation for all it was worth. 'Hey, what do I get outta this deal?' she demanded.

Coco scoffed. 'Why should I give *you* anything?'

Angelica smiled innocently. 'Gee, I dunno. I could axle-dently tell someone why you wanna marry Mr Chuckie's Dad.'

57

Jean-Claude smiled and dished out some more ice cream. 'An extra scoop for cunning.'

Coco shot him a dirty look, then turned back to Angelica with a big phoney smile pasted on her face. 'Tell Auntie Coco what you desire.'

Yes! Angelica sat up straight. She looked around the big fancy office. What could she ask for? More ice cream? More chocolate? Maybe a whole boxful of little tiny plastic high-heeled shoes for her Cynthia doll, so it wouldn't matter when they kept getting lost . . . Hmmm, even *that* didn't seem big enough.

The sound of music drew Angelica's eyes to the window. The Princess Parade was passing by. The princess looked so wonderful, so special, the centre of attention, the star of the whole parade . . .

Suddenly Angelica's eyes lit up. She knew *exactly* what she wanted. Something far better than even a hundred chocolate bars. Better than a million Cynthia shoes.

'Let's see. Not much. Just my own float in the Princess Parade with matching ponies and my own fashion show and to be the flower girl

at your wedding!' Angelica stood up like a princess with her pug nose stuck up in the air. She showed Coco and Jean-Claude just how beautiful she could be for the crowds.

Coco wrinkled her nose in disgust. It was humiliating to make deals with such a spoiled little brat. But Coco would do *anything* to get Mr Yamaguchi's job.

And to do that, she had to convince him that she loved children.

And to do *that*, she had to marry somebody with a kid – fast. She didn't have time to shop around. Chas Finster was her only hope. Let the obnoxious little girl with her stupid pigtails have her silly fifteen minutes of fame. Let her ride in that ridiculous parade, Coco thought. Anything to keep the kid's mouth shut.

'I'll take care of it, Angelique,' Coco said. 'Jean-Claude, find out where our guests are dining tonight.' She grinned slyly. 'Love is on the menu.'

Chapter 10

'This place gots the biggest babies I ever sawed,' Lil whispered.

The babies were with their parents at a singing sumo wrestler restaurant. The 'baby' that Lil saw was really a huge wrestler waiter wearing only a loincloth.

'That's gotta be one stinky nappy,' Phil whispered back.

The group had two tables, one for the grown-ups and one for the children. As soon as the grown-ups were seated, the babies cleared out for some exploring. On the stage a sumo wrestler began his version of the song 'Bad Girls'. Angelica grabbed a second microphone and began to sing a duet with him.

Phil and Lil ran by, grimacing, as they held

their ears. They stopped when they found Chuckie and Tommy.

'And when I seed the magic sprinkles in my hand,' Chuckie was telling Tommy, 'I knowed she was the one.'

'You mean you want the princess to be your new mummy?' Tommy asked.

'Yep!' Chuckie said. 'She's *everything* I been wishin' for. She's real nice. She loves Reptar. And, bestest of all, we can live happily for ever after!'

Across the room a tall figure began pushing through the crowd, nearly knocking people over to get to her target. It was Coco LaBouche. She was headed for the Americans.

Stu had just managed to pick up a piece of sushi with his chopsticks when Coco rushed up to their table.

'Monsieur Pickles!' Coco exclaimed. '*Quelle surprise!*'

'Huh?' Stu was so startled, his chopsticks slipped. 'Whoops . . .' His sushi flipped into the air . . . bounced off Coco's forehead . . . and plopped down the front of her dress.

61

Stu ripped his napkin off and jumped to his feet. 'Oops,' he said. 'I'm sorry. I don't really have the hang of these chopsticks.'

Coco plucked the slimy food out of her dress. She was totally disgusted, but she tried not to show it. 'It's just raw fish . . . on imported *silk*,' she said through clenched teeth. She took a deep breath to calm herself, then put on her most phoney smile.

'Everyone,' Stu said to the others at the table, 'this is Madame LaBouche – '

'Ah-ah-ah!' Coco interrupted in a teasing voice. 'You mean *Mademoiselle.*' She turned her eyes on Chuckie's dad and smiled in exaggerated delight. 'Who is this devastatingly handsome red-haired man you're trying to hide from me?'

Stu looked around. Oh! She was talking about Chas! 'This is my good friend, Chas Finster.'

Coco elbowed Didi out of the way as she squeezed in at the table beside him. *'Enchanté.'*

Chas scooted over to make room. *'Bonsoir,* Mademoiselle – '

'Call me Coco,' she interrupted flirtatiously.

62

She pointed at Chuckie. 'And that adorable misproportioned ragamuffin must be your son.'

'Madame LaBouche?' a woman's voice called out over the noise of the restaurant. 'Madame LaBouche!'

A brief look of irritation passed over Coco's face before she managed to hide it. She turned to see Kira making her way through the crowded restaurant. 'What?' Coco asked, annoyed.

'Hi, Kira,' Chas said.

'I'm sorry to interrupt, Madame,' Kira said politely, 'but these need your signature.' Kira held out a large stack of papers and a pen.

'Can you join us for dinner?' Chas asked.

Kira looked surprised by the invitation. 'Why, I – '

'Oh, you're much too busy, Kira,' Madame LaBouche interrupted. She quickly signed the papers without even glancing at what they said.

As Kira stood by the table, waiting patiently, a little girl peeked out from behind her. She smiled shyly at the other children.

'Oh, that must be Kimi,' Chas said.

'Who?' Coco wondered aloud.

'My *daughter*,' Kira pointedly reminded her boss.

'Oh, of course,' Coco said absently.

'She's a cutie,' Chas said. 'Hey! Do you think Kimi would like to come to the park with me and the kids tomorrow?'

But before Kira could answer, Coco shoved the papers back into her face and answered, 'What a coincidence! I planned to spend the day with her there myself.'

What? Kira couldn't believe it. Her boss had never said a word to Kimi before. 'But, Madame,' she said, 'you never – '

'Tire of taking care of your daughter.' Coco laughed and waved her off. 'But don't thank me now.' She snuggled up close to Chas. 'So it's a date. It'll be just you and me and that adorable swarm of insects – ha, ha – infants.'

While the grown-ups talked, Kimi decided to meet the babies under the table. Her knee-high cowgirl boots clomped on the floor as she toddled over. 'Hi, I'm Kimi. Who're you?'

'I'm Tommy an' that's Phil an' Lil an' Chuckie!'

64

"You're like family to me, Finster.
Name your wish."

"I'd kinda like a new mummy."

"I want that giant tin can *fixed*!
Do you hear me?"

Love at first bite!

"Wow! Reptarland! I've been waiting my entire whole life to see this!"

"Come on! I'll show you a shortcup."

"It's an Ooey-gooey World! It's an Ooey-gooey World!"

"I gots to be brave!"

"Actually, Finster, it's sorta my fault."

"Stop in the name of France, Reptar!"

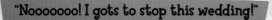

"Nooooooo! I gots to stop this wedding!"

"Chuckie? Would you like to dance with
your new mummy?"

'Hello!' Chuckie said, admiring her boots.

'So, Kimi, do you live in Reptarland?' Tommy asked.

Kimi laughed. 'No, me and my mum live in the city. But I get to come all the time 'cause my mummy works here.'

'Have you seen the princess?' Chuckie asked hopefully.

'Does Reptar have dragon breath?' she joked.

'Huh?' Chuckie said.

Kimi led them to the restaurant's front window. She pointed way off in the distance. 'The princess lives up there in the castle on the bowlcano and comes out between 'splosions.'

Off in the distance a Japanese-style castle rose from the side of a mountain-like volcano. The babies oohed and aahed.

'Now we know where to find your new princess mum, Chuckie,' Tommy said.

Tommy noticed Chuckie's fearful stare. 'Chuckie?'

'Sorry,' Chuckie said. 'I stopped listening after 'splosions.'

65

Chuckie and his friends looked back out of the window. Chuckie gasped. The volcano was erupting! Fire spewed into the sky! Chuckie couldn't believe it. The princess lived on top of a fire-breathing volcano!

Wow, thought Chuckie. The princess isn't just beautiful and magical. She also must be very brave!

That settled it.

The princess would make a *perfect* mummy. I will have to go and ask her, Chuckie thought. There was only one problem.

How could he get to her castle?

Chapter 11

The following day the babies and their parents were at a giant warehouse at the back of Reptarland.

Above their heads, a man's legs dangled out of Reptar's jaws. But he wasn't being eaten. He was a repairman. He was working inside the mechanical Reptar's head.

'Why didn't you people just follow my design?' Stu asked the workers. 'I used paper clips and rubber bands for a reason!' He shook his head and whispered to Didi, 'I love their fries and everything, but this is advanced robotics.'

The robot that Stu Pickles had made for Reptarland towered into the rafters of the big warehouse. Several ladders leaned against the robot so workers could reach it to fix it.

Down below Stu sat at a high-tech panel with buttons, switches and a microphone. Lying on the ground around him were special helmets, gloves and boots. The other grown-ups and their babies were gathered around to watch.

'It looks pretty complicated,' Chas said.

'Actually, it's not,' Stu said. 'You put on the gear. Then, anything you do, Reptar does.'

Stu put on a glove and waved.

The giant mechanical Reptar waved.

The grown-ups oohed and aahed.

'It's so simple, a child could work it.' Stu smiled at Tommy and put the helmet on him. 'Right, champ?' he said, and nodded.

Tommy didn't understand the grown-up words. But it always seemed to make his daddy happy when he nodded back. Tommy nodded his head. The giant Reptar nodded too.

That was a mistake. The worker inside the Reptar head slipped and tumbled out!

Stu snatched the helmet off Tommy's head. 'Oops! It's not really a children's toy.'

Then Coco LaBouche swept into the room,

dragging Kimi by the hand. Chuckie watched Coco carefully. Something about her made his tummy feel funny. Kimi didn't seem too crazy about her, either. She pulled free from Coco's too-tight grasp and walked over to say hello to her new friends.

'Hey, Kimi,' Tommy said. 'Is that the same Robosnail as in the video?' He pointed at another giant robot that stood behind Reptar. It had a huge curved shell.

'That's Robosnail, all right,' Kimi explained. 'He fought Reptar.'

'*Bonjour,* everyone!' Coco called. 'How's my resident genius?' she asked Stu.

But before he could even answer, Coco had turned all her attention to Chuckie's dad. 'Ready to go, *mon chéri?*'

Chas smiled. 'Let me just get Dilly settled.'

Chas was wearing a soft baby carrier strapped on to his chest. Didi helped buckle Dil into the carrier.

Coco leaned in and smiled playfully at Dil. 'And how is this precious gherkin today?'

Chas smiled at the surprising, remarkable

69

Frenchwoman at his side. Coco seemed to be *really* good with children.

Dil bonked Coco on the head with his rattle.

Coco gasped and rubbed her head. 'Well, you're just a lawsuit waiting to happen, aren't you?'

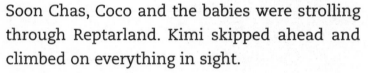

Soon Chas, Coco and the babies were strolling through Reptarland. Kimi skipped ahead and climbed on everything in sight.

'Mon *chéri,*' Coco said to Chas, squeezing his arm, 'I could listen to your fascinating health history all day.'

Wow, Chas thought. None of his other dates had said anything like that! 'I'll tell you all about my poor sinus drainage when I get back from the little boys' room. Would you mind holding Dil?'

'Of course not.' Coco held out her hands and took the squirming baby. But as soon as Chas disappeared in the men's room, she quickly held Dil out at arm's length, as if his nappy needed changing.

Pfthhh! Dil let her know what he thought of her too, with a great big raspberry.

Coco needed help – and she needed it now! Lucky for her, she'd planned for everything. Scowling at the drooling baby, she quickly adjusted a microphone and earpiece that were hidden in her large U-shaped earring. It was her secret link to her office. Chas didn't know Coco was wearing it.

Coco had no idea how to deal with children. So she had come up with a brilliant idea. She had arranged for Kira to be stationed in Coco's office. They could talk by way of a hidden microphone. Kira could see Coco, Chas and the children on the TV monitors linked to the building's security system.

'Kira,' Coco whispered frantically into the microphone, 'they're staring at me, and this one is leaking from the mouth! What do I do?'

'Just smile and be nice,' Kira instructed her.

Coco glared at the baby in her hands. 'Hello, you are not horrible.'

Dil kicked and wiggled. He grabbed Coco's lips.

71

'Ah! Let go! Do you know how much I paid for these lips?'

Tommy frowned. 'I don't think Dil likes that lady too much, you guys,' he whispered.

'I don't think she likes Dil too much, either,' Chuckie whispered to Tommy.

'She's not a nice lady,' Lil announced. 'She's too pointy.'

'And her shoes don't match that outfit,' Phil added. The others nodded in agreement.

Dil began to fuss. Coco searched for his dummy, but couldn't find it. Tommy and the others went over and tugged on Coco's clothes. Dil began to cry.

'Kira!' Coco cried into the microphone. 'He's crying! What do I do now?'

'Comfort him,' Kira said. 'Gently bounce him up and down.'

With an exasperated shrug, Coco jiggled the baby up and down.

Blechhh!

'All right, Dilly!' Phil cheered.

The milk that was *in* Dil came back *out* just as Chas came back. Coco gasped in horror and

quickly handed the baby over to him.

Chas smiled and dabbed Dil's face clean. 'Awww. According to Dr Lipschitz, the famous child psychologist, Dilly just gave you a gift.'

Coco forced a smile and tried to ignore the smell. 'Why wouldn't he? After all, children are my life.'

Chas's eyes lit up. He couldn't believe his ears. 'Oh! I have that poem taped to the refrigerator!'

Coco stared at him. 'Pardon?'

'"Children Are My Life"!' Kira hissed at her boss through the headphones. 'It's a classic!'

Chas began to recite it. '"Dappled laughter/ padding feet . . ."'

Delighted, Kira said the next line into the microphone. Only Coco could hear, through her secret headphone. '"Joy and wonder/Heaven's treat." It's one of my favourites,' Kira added.

Coco looked as if she was going to imitate Dil – and throw up. But she dutifully repeated: '"Joy and wonder/Heaven's treat." It's one of my favourites.'

'Wow . . .' Chas breathed. He had never met

another person who knew his favourite poem by heart. He gazed at Coco, enchanted. The children began to tug on his clothes.

'Oh, dear,' Chas said. 'They're getting fussy.'

Coco heard Kira through her hidden microphone: 'Why don't you take them to Ooey-gooey World?'

Coco looked mortified. 'Ooey-gooey World!'

'Ooey-gooey World?' Chas exclaimed. 'What a great idea!'

Oh, no! Coco thought helplessly. Anything but that!

Chapter 12

Chas grinned as he helped Coco step into the colourful little cars. He couldn't believe she had suggested the Ooey-gooey World ride. A lot of big kids couldn't stand it. A lot of grown-ups thought it was corny. But Chas loved it because he knew Chuckie loved it.

The little cars went down a miniature railway in a tunnel inside the mountain. Along the way, happy wooden puppets waved and sang along with scratchy, piped-in music. The ride was named for the sticky, jelly-like goo that oozed from the walls of the tunnel and piled up in blobs along the tracks.

Chas shook his head in wonder at the amazing Coco LaBouche. How did she know that the Ooey-gooey ride was so perfect, when she had no small children of her own? She

seemed to have a natural talent for making little children happy.

But Chas had no idea Coco was actually having a miserable time. She stared in disgust at an Ooey-gooey World worker wearing a gaudy costume and name tag. 'Kira,' Coco hissed into her microphone when Chas wasn't listening, 'remind me to fire whoever wrote this hideous song.'

Chas and Coco sat in the front section of the car, with Dil between them. The other babies sat behind them. They laughed and giggled in delight as the car began to move slowly down a small dip in the track.

Chas lifted his arms high in the air, as if flying down the steepest hill on the scariest roller-coaster. 'Look, no hands! Wheeeeee!'

Coco had never been more miserable. 'How could you have suggested this thing?' she whispered into her microphone.

'Excuse me?' Chas asked.

'Oh! I said, uh . . . this song makes me want to sing!'

Uh-oh. That was the wrong thing to say.

Now Chas wanted her to sing along with him to the Ooey-gooey theme song. 'It's an Ooey-gooey World, it's an Ooey-gooey World . . .'

Dil bonked his rattle in time to the music – on Coco's head. Coco tried not to gag.

Lil leaned out of the car and grabbed a handful of goo. 'Ooh, it's so soft and squishy-ful.'

Phil grabbed a wad off her hand and stuck it in his nappy as he said, 'That's good stuff. Let's stock up.' As he grabbed more handfuls of the goo, some of the globs hit Chuckie's glasses.

'And eggsackly how'm I s'posed to find the princess with my glassies all googlied up?' Chuckie wailed.

Kimi grabbed Dil's bottle and squirted Chuckie in the face to try to clean his glasses.

'Thank you – I guess,' Chuckie said.

As the car moved around the bend, Tommy spotted something. 'Look, guys! The castle! C'mon! Let's go and see that princess, Chuckie!'

Chuckie held on tight to the side of the wobbling car. 'You guys!' Chuckie called anxiously. 'They said to keep your hands and feets inside at all times.'

'Uh . . . that didn't stop her!' Phil pointed out. All the babies gasped. Kimi had crawled out of the back of the slow-moving car. Now she was crawling off along the rails!

'Come on!' Kimi called out. 'I'll show you the shortcup.'

'Kimi! No!' Chuckie called after her.

Tommy, Phil and Lil scrambled out of the car.

'What are you waiting for?' Kimi shouted back.

'Oh, great,' Chuckie moaned.

'C'mon, Chuckie!' Kimi said. 'You can do it!'

Chuckie groaned. That's what his best friend, Tommy, always said. Tommy was an adventurer – a baby who wanted to see the world. Chuckie was the kind of kid who was happy to stay in his own little world, in his sandbox in his own back garden. But that meant he often got left behind.

Chuckie stared at the scary tracks. He gazed at the castle on the distant volcano, where the princess lived. He remembered how it sometimes spewed fire. Shivering, Chuckie sat all the way back in his seat in the Ooey-gooey

car. It was safer to stay put.

But Tommy and Kimi and Phil and Lil were going on without him. What if they found the princess? Would they give her Chuckie's message?

No. It was something he needed to tell her himself.

I gots to be brave, Chuckie told himself. Like Tommy. If I don't, I might mess up my chance to get a new mummy for ever!

Bracing himself, he took a deep breath, squeezed Wawa tight and then leaped out of the slow-moving car.

Kira had just stepped out for a quick cup of coffee. Listening to the Ooey-gooey World theme song over and over through Coco's secret microphone had made her sleepy. As she came back into Coco's office, she glanced at the TV monitors – and nearly dropped her coffee!

The children!

Or, more accurately – *no* children! She couldn't see them *anywhere* on any of the TV monitors.

'My Kimi!' she exclaimed into Coco's microphone. 'Madame, the babies are *gone!*'

Coco whirled around. Oh, no! It was true! The back seat of her Ooey-gooey car was completely empty.

Coco groaned. The little monsters! How in the world had they managed to slip away? Now what? She glanced at Chas. Luckily, he hadn't realized that the babies were missing yet. He was too busy telling her about his top ten allergy attacks of the decade. Carefully, so he wouldn't notice, she whispered into her microphone earring, 'Get them *back* before Wheezy finds out!'

Frantically Kira snatched up the phone on Coco's desk. 'Security? We have an emergency situation! Five babies are lost in the park!'

Chapter 13

'Kimi?' Tommy asked. 'Are you sure you know how to get to the castle?'

'Do I know how to get to the castle?' Kimi scoffed. A low, rumbling sound came from the volcano. Tommy shivered. 'We gots to hurry!' Kimi shouted. 'When the volcano makes that noise, the princess comes out of her castle!'

A Reptarland Security Guard Ninja was following their movements on a video monitor. 'We've located the babies in Sector Twelve,' he radioed in.

The babies followed Kimi through the tunnels of Ooey-gooey World, under a big dragon boat swing, across shooting geysers, over a water lily pond with fake crocodiles, past samurai warriors and down a giant corkscrew slide to the base of the volcano.

'It looks kind of scary, Tommy,' Chuckie called along the way. 'I'm not jumping down there! No way! I'm not – '

Phil pushed Chuckie on to a moving platform.

'Thanks, I needed that,' Chuckie said.

The babies continued to forge ahead through dark and scary tunnels. At the base of the volcano, they found a large lift and stepped inside. Finally they stumbled up to the gates of the castle.

Kimi grinned proudly. 'I told ya I knowed a shortcup!'

'Maybe next time you can show it to us,' Phil wheezed, out of breath.

Suddenly the doors to the castle opened and the princess emerged.

'She's so prettiful!' Lil gasped.

The princess smoothly turned their way and froze for a few seconds. The babies admired her beautiful face. Then she waved her arm and turned away with a jerk and wobbled quickly back inside the castle.

'Oh, no!' Chuckie said, his eyes filling with tears. 'She's gone!' Chuckie didn't know this

princess was a robot. And neither did any of the other babies.

'Go get her, Chuckie,' Tommy said, patting his friend's shoulder. 'She's right inside.'

'You're right, Tommy,' Chuckie exclaimed. 'I'm gonna do it.' Chuckie took a few steps towards the castle door and stopped. 'But what if she doesn't like me?'

'Go on, Chuckie,' Tommy urged. 'You'll never know unless you try.'

Suddenly the castle door slammed and the face of a huge dragon was staring right at Chuckie. Not a real dragon, of course. It was a huge door knocker made to look like a scary dragon face. But to Chuckie, it seemed to be growling like a vicious beast and he backed away. 'Nice doggie . . .' Chuckie stammered.

Then something even scarier happened.

Reptarland Security Guard Ninjas surrounded him and the others. They didn't speak. They just grabbed the babies and carried them wiggling and squirming down the side of the volcano.

Where are they taking us? Chuckie wondered. Will I ever see the princess again?

Will I ever see my daddy again?

The Ninjas took the babies back inside the Ooey-gooey ride through a side door. They hid by the tracks and waited for the sound of a car. Chuckie waited to be thrown on to the tracks.

Instead, the Ninjas waited for the car to reach their hiding place. Then they quietly slipped the babies inside, back into their old seats behind Chas and Coco.

Chas never even noticed they were gone!

'At least we didn't have to walk back,' Phil said.

Chuckie sighed. 'Now I'm never gonna meet the princess. I blowed my chance because I was too big a scaredy-cat.'

'Don't worry, Chuckie,' Lil said. 'You'll get your new mummy.'

Suddenly the car made a sharp turn. Chuckie felt himself being thrown out of his seat. He grabbed the closest thing he could – Coco's hand. Coco turned around and stared at Chuckie. With a fake smile, she said, 'Look, *mon chéri*. I think he likes me!'

A delighted Chas smiled back.

84

Chapter 14

The City of Light twinkled in the night. Accordion music floated on the evening breeze.

Spike, Tommy's dog, wandered the curving Paris streets, sniffing for the scent of his Pickles family. As he passed a café, his nose caught a delicious smell. Food!

Spike was hungry. The café owner saw the lonely dog and smiled. '*Viens ici, chéri* . . . come here . . . *oui, c'est ça.*'

Spike didn't understand French words any better than he understood English words. But he heard the sound of kindness in the man's voice. Spike wagged his tail as the man tossed him some scraps of food – cheese, croissants and pizza. '*Bon appétit, petit chien!*'

Spike began to wolf down the delicious food. Then he stopped.

A beautiful French poodle stood in a pool of light from a corner streetlamp. She took a few shy steps towards him.

Spike nudged a slice of pizza toward her with his nose.

The poodle politely nudged it back.

For a moment both dogs stared at the slice of pizza. Then they wagged their tails and bit into opposite ends. Slowly they chewed, pulling the stringy cheese between them like rubber bands, tighter and tighter, until finally – *whack!* – it snapped and smacked their heads together, cheek to cheek.

Chas had returned to the hotel with the babies. He had no idea that they'd been on just about every exciting ride in the park – without him. He took them upstairs to find their parents.

'So, Chas, how was your date?' Stu asked as they came inside.

Chas blushed and toyed with his bow tie. 'Wonderful! Coco and I have so much in

common!' He counted on his fingers. 'We're both lactose intolerant, love kids, and she finds bureaucrats fascinating!'

'Who doesn't, you babe magnet!' Betty teased.

But Didi wasn't so enthusiastic. After all, they were in a foreign country and he'd only just met Coco. 'Just be careful, Charles. I wouldn't want you to rush into anything.'

'Don't worry,' Chas said. 'I'm not going to make any rash decisions. First, I have to see how Coco and my little Chuckie get along. He and I are a team, you know.'

Moonlight shone on Chuckie's face as he lay in bed next to Tommy that night. He and his friends had had an adventure. But it was no thanks to Chuckie. As always, he'd only gone because his best friend, Tommy, dragged him along. It was kind of embarrassing.

'Tommy?' Chuckie said softly.

Tommy yawned. 'Yeah, Chuckie?'

'Do you think someone like me could ever

learn to be brave like you an' my daddy an' Reptar?'

'Sure.'

'But how, Tommy?' Chuckie asked.

'Well, um . . .' Tommy thought hard. 'Maybe you could try thinkin' of somethin' else next time you feel a-scared.'

Chuckie sighed. 'I tried once, but I just thought of somethin' scarier.'

Tommy yawned again. 'Why don'tcha try thinkin' 'bout stuff that makes you feel good?'

'You mean like my Happy Hippo blankie or my favourite moon rock or my Wawa . . . ?'

'Uh-huh.' Tommy's eyes began to droop. Soon he nodded off to sleep.

'Or a new mummy,' Chuckie said. Then he pulled the covers up to his nose and hugged Wawa the bear. 'Next time I see the princess,' he whispered to Wawa, 'I'm gonna be brave.'

The door to the room creaked open. Chas tiptoed in to check on the boys. He patted Tommy, then tenderly kissed Chuckie good night. 'Sweet dreams, Chuckie,' he whispered.

Chuckie smiled. He knew his dreams would

88

be sweet that night. He was sure he'd dream about his new mummy.

✦　　　✦　　　✦

In the connecting room, Chas sat on his bed humming as he pulled off his shoes.

His eyes fell on something gold and shiny on his pillow. Puzzled, he picked it up. 'What's this? A gold inhaler? Gee, most hotels just leave mints.' Then he saw that there were some words engraved on the side. He looked closer and read: CHAD, YOU TAKE MY BREATH AWAY. FOREVER YOURS, COCO.

Chas sighed dreamily. A present from that wonderful Coco. Then he sat up with a start. 'Chad?'

✦　　　✦　　　✦

Chuckie was walking down a long, dark hall. Eerie music and evil laughter echoed off the walls. He walked up a flight of stairs. Scary warriors stood guard.

'H-hello?' Chuckie stammered nervously. 'Where am I?'

His eyes fell on a dragon-shaped door knocker.

'Ahhhhh . . . ' he moaned, and backed away.

The warriors closed in.

'I gots to be brave, I gots to be brave, I gots to be brave . . . but why'd I have to pick today?' Chuckie muttered.

Then Chuckie changed. His hands and feet became stronger, like hammers. Every nerve tingled. He was a master of martial arts – Chuckie Chan!

'Hi-yah!' He threw off the guards with an outrageous series of lightning-fast kicks and chops and headed for the castle door.

Suddenly the dragon door knocker morphed into a real dragon!

'Hi-yah!' Chuckie flipped the beast over his shoulder and yanked open the door. A white light blinded him. Somehow he knew that what he sought lay within that shining light.

Bravely, Chuckie reached forward. Then he felt a hand grab his shoulder.

Someone was yanking him! Someone was pulling him through the air!

Chapter 15

'Chuck-a-roo! Chuckie! You gots to get ready!'

It was Tommy. Chuckie had been dreaming. They were in bed in the hotel.

'Angelica says we're going to get to see the princess in a show with Reptar,' Lil said.

'This could be your chance, Chuckie!' Tommy said.

'I'm gonna meet the princess?' Chuckie asked.

'Yup,' Tommy replied.

'I'm gonna meet the princess! I'm gonna meet the princess!' Chuckie cried as he ran through the hotel suite. Suddenly he stopped. 'Gee, maybe I should take her a present.'

'You want a princess to be your mum? But what about Coco?' Angelica asked.

'Who?' the babies asked together.

'Mr Chuckie's Dad's girlfriend!' Angelica explained impatiently. 'The Reptarland lady!'

'But that mean lady's not the princess, Angelica,' Tommy said.

'Yeah,' Chuckie said. 'I'm gonna get the real princess for my mummy.'

'Lissen up, babies!' Angelica said. 'I'm supposed to ride in my own parade on a float with lots of pink tarnations and ponies, and you better not mess it up for me!' She stormed out of the room.

The babies looked at one another and shrugged. They had no idea what she was talking about.

'I know somebody who needs a nap,' Phil muttered.

She's beautiful, Chuckie thought later that morning. He clutched his bear and gazed at the lovely face on the poster. And this is only a pitcher of her!

He, Tommy, Phil, Lil and Angelica and the grown-ups were in the theatre foyer waiting for

92

the *Princess Spectacular* to begin.

Suddenly Coco breezed in. She ran over to greet Chas, Betty, Howard, Stu and Didi, who was holding Dil. She gave them all air kisses – kisses that didn't make it all the way to the grown-ups' cheeks. '*Bonjour, mes amis!*' Coco exclaimed. 'Let me show you to your seats.'

Stu smiled – but Coco breezed past him to link arms with Chas. Chattering non-stop, she led him down to front-row seats. Stu and the others followed.

The babies were so excited! They were going to see the princess and Reptar!

Coco held her arms out to Chuckie. 'And how is Coco's favourite boy?'

But Chuckie didn't want one of her air kisses. He didn't want to feel one of her awkward hugs around him. He scrambled past her to take his seat.

'He must be excited about the show,' Chas apologized.

Coco studied the little red-haired boy perched on the edge of his seat. The dad was easy to fool. But the little boy was going to be a

tougher sell. Maybe if – *eww!* – she held him on her lap.

Coco felt a yank on her sleeve. 'Hi, Mr Chuckie's Dad's girlfriend,' Angelica said brightly. Then she winked and whispered, 'How's my float comin' along?'

'Fabulous,' Coco said. Promise the little squirt anything, she thought, and maybe she'll leave me alone. 'We're just waiting for the imported ponies.'

Angelica bit her lip. 'And I still get the float if Mr Chuckie's Dad marries a princess 'stead of you, right?' she asked nervously.

'Yes, yes, yes,' Coco said impatiently, not really listening. She pulled away from the child's grasp. 'Now, please, I really must – '

Coco froze as Angelica's words sank in. 'What? Why did you ask me that?'

Angelica shrugged as if it were no big deal. 'Um, the Finster kid wants a princess for a mum. And let's face it, lady, *you're* no princess.'

Angelica dashed off.

'Not a princess? Harumph!' Coco said indignantly. 'My little commoner, if the tiara

94

fits, wear it.' Coco's eyes narrowed in determination. She left the Americans at the show and marched out of the auditorium. She had an idea.

In the auditorium the lights went down. Music began to play. The squirming babies fell silent and still with their eyes glued to the stage.

An announcer's voice boomed: 'Ladies and gentlemen, emperors and empresses, welcome to the *Princess Spectacular!*'

The babies bounced in their seats and clapped their hands as the rest of the crowd began to applaud. Kira and Kimi slipped into some empty seats behind them. Chas glanced over his shoulder and gave Kira a little wave. Kira waved back. Kimi climbed over the back of the seats so she could sit with the other babies.

The *Princess Spectacular* began with a fight between Reptar and Robosnail. Reptar bared his metal teeth and roared. Robosnail charged and slashed with his claws. Reptar won and then stomped through a Japanese village. Bamboo houses were crushed beneath his feet as if they were made of matchsticks. A princess

95

appeared in the spotlight, wearing a flowered kimono and covering her face with a fan. She looked as beautiful as a bouquet; even Reptar stopped and stared. She sang a song, then stroked the dinosaur on the cheek.

Enthralled, Chuckie offered the princess his teddy bear. She accepted it with a small bow. The last note of the beautiful music played. And then came the surprise ending.

The princess lowered her Japanese fan and smiled. She smiled right at Chuckie sitting in the front row.

Chuckie gasped! He tried to yank his bear back. Oh, no! This was horrible! A nightmare!

His beautiful princess was really... Madame Coco LaBouche in disguise!

The babies were stunned. Dil's dummy popped out in surprise. Chuckie was still tugging at one of Wawa's arms, while Coco clung just as tightly to the other arm.

'Wow, Chuckie's sharing Wawa,' Chas uttered, completely spellbound.

Kira couldn't believe her eyes. 'Madame LaBouche?'

'*That* lady's the princess?' Lil exclaimed.

Tommy shook his head. 'But she *can't* be!'

'Bravo!' Chas clapped loudly as he leaped to his feet. 'Isn't she talented?' He glanced down at his son, who seemed just as awestruck as he did.

With a lovesick sigh, Chas turned to Stu and Didi. 'Gosh, you guys,' he blurted out. 'I think Chuckie and I are both in love.'

Then he ran up and took a picture of the 'princess' and Chuckie as they pulled at opposite ends of Chuckie's teddy bear.

Chapter 16

Three days went by. Chas was hooked and Madame LaBouche was happy to reel him in. Now she had lined everybody up in front of the camera to have a group picture taken.

'Say *brie!*' the photographer shouted.

'*Brie!*' everyone said.

Flash!

The babies and the grown-ups were all dressed up in their fancy clothes, just like at Grandpa Lou's wedding. They were in their hotel room, squeezed into a tight bunch. They were posing for a group photo, so Chas could remember the moment for all time.

Flash!

The photographer took another picture of them. '*Merci!*' he said, then left the room.

The children and their parents helped

themselves to a tray of French pastries, *café au lait* and fresh orange juice. It was a special breakfast for a special day – Chas Finster's wedding day! He was getting married to Coco LaBouche!

Chuckie tugged on his bow tie. It was too tight. His fancy suit was really uncomfortable. And his dad had slicked back his hair. He stood up straight and tall. 'How do I look?' Chuckie asked.

'Extra-specially hamsome, Chuckie!' Tommy said with a smile.

'Yeah,' Phil agreed. ''Cept for them funny clothes and the slimy stuff in your hair.'

Lil poked him in the ribs.

'Ow! What'd I say?' Phil exclaimed.

Chuckie made a face and messed up his hair real good till it was back to normal – sticking up.

Lil picked up some drippy eggs from the floor. 'Here, we saved you some scramblied eggs, Chuckie.'

'Uh, no thanks, Lil,' Chuckie replied. 'I kind of like 'em better on a plate.' Then he turned to the others.

99

'Well, guys,' he said, trying to smile. 'This is the day I been waitin' for. It sure is gonna be great havin' a princess mum.' He looked hopefully at all his friends. 'Isn't it?'

'A'course, Chuckie,' Tommy said.

Chuckie frowned. 'Then how come I don't feel so good?'

'Well, uh . . . ' Tommy said, adjusting Chuckie's tie. 'Maybe this thing is too tight. Don't worry, Chuck-a-roo. Everything's gonna be okay.'

Stalking a fly, Phil pulled the tablecloth on the food cart, spilling everything on to the floor.

Coco came into the room and scowled. 'Do you see those sticky fingers?' she complained to Jean-Claude and Kira. 'Jam-covered mouths? Guilty little faces? Disinfect them!'

The babies looked at each other. Chuckie hugged Wawa tight.

Angelica chimed in, 'Can't you klutzy babies do anything right?'

Suddenly Coco looked as if she'd just smelled one of Dil's used nappies. 'What are you doing with that mangy thing? Give me that this instant!'

Chuckie shook his head and tightened his hold on Wawa. None of this made sense. The princess was supposed to be kind. The princess loved Reptar – at least, in the story. How could she hate a sweet old teddy bear like Wawa?

Coco snarled and took a step closer to Chuckie. 'How *dare* you defy me!'

She grabbed the bear and tugged. Chuckie tugged back. Back and forth they yanked on poor old Wawa. The babies gathered around. One by one they grabbed on behind Chuckie. They pulled and pulled.

Whoa! Coco LaBouche was strong!

Finally Coco gave one last yank. Chuckie and his friends tumbled backward. As they fell, they bumped into a table. A vase crashed to the floor and splashed them all with water.

Kira had had enough. She stepped forward to help the babies to their feet and wiped them off with a napkin.

But Coco was furious. 'Ah! That vase is worth more than all of you put together!' she screamed. 'Jean-Claude, take those wretched

dust mops away. I will *not* have them ruining my wedding day!'

All right! Angelica thought. Finally somebody else besides her understood how annoying those dumb babies could be! She liked the way this lady bossed people around. 'Looks like you dumb babies are going to miss the wedding!'

'And Jean-Claude,' Coco added, 'don't forget the Big Mouth too!'

'Hey!' Angelica cried.

Jean-Claude picked up Dil, grabbed Angelica around the waist, and began to herd the other babies towards the door. Angelica kicked her legs. She pounded her fists against Jean-Claude's shoulder. 'What do you think you're doing? I'm the flower girl!' She kicked Jean-Claude's shins.

'I feel your pain, Mademoiselle,' Jean-Claude said, 'but unfortunately you just got *le boot*.' He dragged the children out the door.

'But what about my float?' Angelica protested. 'And the imported ponies? And . . .'

They disappeared out of the door.

Kira watched them go with a troubled look

102

on her face. She was a quiet woman. She did her job well and she rarely complained – even working for a tough boss like Coco. But this time she couldn't hold her tongue. 'Madame LaBouche!' she protested.

'Burn this hideous moth-eaten rabbit,' Coco told Kira, shoving Chuckie's teddy bear into her arms. 'I *never* want to see it again.'

With that she stormed out of the room.

Kira looked into the eyes of the old worn bear. Poor Chas. Poor Chuckie! she thought as she slowly followed her boss out of the door. They had no idea what they were getting themselves into.

Chapter 17

Coco was waiting impatiently by the time Kira got to the limousine. Without a word, Kira slipped into the back seat beside her boss.

'To Notre Dame!' Coco yelled at the driver. '*Tout de suite!*' The limo quickly pulled away into the busy Paris traffic.

Coco didn't bother to make small talk with Kira. She simply stared out of the window at the traffic, impatiently tapping her foot on the carpeted limo floor.

Kira fidgeted nervously. She felt awful. She felt as if she were being hurled towards an event that only she could see would be a total disaster.

Someone should say something, she thought. Someone should try to stop this wedding from taking place.

She thought of Chas and his funny little moustache. He was the sweetest man she had ever met. She'd never known a man who loved children as much as she did.

And Chuckie – adorable Chuckie. A little boy any woman would be proud to have for a son. Kira's heart ached. Chuckie deserved a mother who would hold him when he cried. Who would hold his hand when he crossed the road. Who would read him stories and chase the monsters away and play with him when he was lonely. Who would love him for ever.

She looked at the woman sitting beside her. Coco LaBouche wasn't a mummy. She was a fire-breathing monster!

I have to stop her, Kira realized.

'Madame LaBouche,' Kira began, 'I don't know why you're doing this, but it's obvious you don't really care about Chas or Chuckie.'

Coco frowned. 'Which is which again?'

Kira couldn't believe it! *I can't let her do this! I can't let her ruin Chas and Chuckie's life!*

'I can no longer stand by and watch you destroy their lives. I'm telling Chas the truth,'

105

Kira declared. 'And there's not a thing you can do to stop me.'

The driver screeched to a halt. The back door opened. And Coco shoved Kira out of the car. 'Except throw you out on the kerb,' Coco said. '*Au revoir!*'

Kira gasped as she tumbled into the street and the limo tore off.

Coco caught a glimpse of Kira reflected in her make-up mirror, through the rear window. She was running after the car. 'Looks like our little mouse is up for the chase – and in high heels,' she muttered. Then to the driver she said, 'Step on it! There's no time to waste.'

Chapter 18

'I'm sorry, guys,' Chuckie said. 'If I didn't want a princess mummy so bad, we wouldn't be in this terrible place.'

The babies were on the other side of the city in the Reptarland warehouse, shivering on the cold, hard floor. Jean-Claude had brought them there and now he sat beneath a single bare light bulb reading the newspaper. Behind him stood the giant Reptar and equally giant Robosnail.

'It's not so terrible, Chuckie,' Tommy said brightly. 'At least we gots Reptar to keep us company.'

'Well, I've decided I don't want a princess mummy no more,' Chuckie declared. 'I don't needs magic and sparkly dust. Alls I wants is a real mummy like you guys gots, who smiles

and talks nice to me and tucks me in at night and tells me stories' – tears rolled down his cheeks – 'and who loves me.'

Chuckie buried his face in his arms and began to sob. His friends looked sadly at one another.

Angelica went over and sat down next to Chuckie. 'Oh, c'mon, Finster. Don't cry.'

'I can't help it, Angelica,' Chuckie said. 'I feel bad. My daddy's marrying a lady who doesn't like me or my Wawa or my friends.' He sniffled. 'And it's all my fault.'

No one knew what to say.

Phil looked at the others and shrugged. 'When he's right, he's right.'

And then Angelica did something that was very difficult for her. She confessed. 'Actually, Finster, it's sorta my fault.'

Tommy stood up and toddled over to her. 'What do you mean, Angelica?'

Angelica looked at her shoes to avoid their stares. 'Well, um . . . lessee, where shall I start? It's like this.' She cleared her throat, then said, 'Mr Yummy-sushi was on TV and he told the

French lady you can't have joy if you don't have a heart. Well, she had one in a jar, but she still needed a spiny man with a kid, so I told her how you wanted a princess mum, and she was s'posed to give me my own pony float' – she took a deep breath – 'but she made the whole thing up.'

All the babies stared at her. They had no idea what she was talking about. Angelica frowned and grunted at them for not understanding. Then she heaved a big sigh and tried to make it simple. 'I helped that lady trick your daddy into marrying her,' Angelica said.

Now they got it.

'You did?' Chuckie cried. 'But – '

'Bad! Yucky! Bad!' Baby Dil scolded.

'Pipe down, drooly,' Angelica snapped.

Dil blew her a raspberry.

'Dilly's right. That's one of the worstest things you ever done,' Tommy said.

'Awright, awright,' Angelica said. 'I know it was bad – even for me. But sometimes I just can't help myself.' She looked at Chuckie. 'I'm sorry, Chuckie.'

109

Chuckie stuck his fingers behind his glasses and scrubbed the tears out of his eyes. What Angelica did wasn't very nice, but at least she'd apologized. The bigger meanie here was Coco LaBouche.

'You guys, I can't let that lady marry my daddy! It's like you always say, Tommy. A baby's gotta do what a baby's gotta do! And we gots to stop that wedding!'

'How're you gonna do that, Chuckie?' Tommy said.

'Actually, I was hoping you had an idea, Tommy,' Chuckie said.

Tommy looked up at the giant Reptar. 'Hmm. I think I do! Angelica, do you still know how to tie shoes?'

Chapter 19

'Oh, Betty, Notre Dame!' Didi exclaimed as she gazed in awe at the beautiful old church.

'Eh, seen one church, you've seen 'em all,' Betty said with a shrug. 'Wake me if you spot a hunchback.'

Notre Dame Cathedral was the oldest church in Paris. Its Gothic towers pointed towards the heavens. Sunlight streamed in through its stained-glass windows and cast colourful patterns on the tiled floor. Wedding guests found seats in the front rows of the church.

Phil and Lil's dad, Howard, had his video camera ready to film every moment of the wedding. Stu was best man. He stood up at the front of the church with Chas. Stu sniffed back a tear. Weddings always made him cry.

Chas looked around the church. It was quiet. Too quiet. Obviously there were no children in the whole building. 'I wonder where Chuckie is,' Chas said with a worried frown. 'I wouldn't want him to miss any of the excitement.'

Chuckie definitely wasn't missing the excitement. He was right in the middle of it. Back in the warehouse, he and the other babies had found the gear that went with Stu's mechanical Reptar: the helmet, the gloves and the boots.

They glanced at Jean-Claude. *Good!* His nose was still buried in the newspaper. He wasn't expecting any problems from a handful of babies.

'Okay, guys,' Chuckie whispered. 'You know the plan.' He nodded his head towards Jean-Claude. 'Angelica, you keep him busy while we get inside Reptar.'

'You got it, Finster,' Angelica replied.

The babies toddled off. One by one Chuckie, Tommy, Phil, Lil and Kimi climbed up into

112

Reptar's giant head. Meanwhile Angelica snickered as she tiptoed over to Jean-Claude. She froze when the newspaper rustled.

But he was only turning the page.

Whew! Angelica reached down and untied his shoes. Then she retied them. Only this time she tied the two shoes together.

Jean-Claude peeked over the top of the paper. '*What* do you think you're doing?' he demanded.

Angelica gulped. 'Oh, I'm just, uh . . . practisin' tyin' shoes!' She gave him one of her famous 'Little Miss Innocent' smiles.

Jean-Claude rolled his eyes and went back to reading his paper. 'Children are *so* easily amused.'

Angelica snickered. Grown-ups are so easily fooled!

By now the babies had climbed, unnoticed, into the huge mechanical Reptar. The little room inside the top of Reptar's head was just like the cockpit of an aeroplane. Chuckie sat down at the control panel. The other babies clustered around him.

'So, how do you make this thing go?' Phil wondered.

Chuckie chewed his bottom lip. 'I'm not sure eggsackly.' Hesitantly he poked one of the buttons. A video screen lit up.

The babies looked closer. They could see Angelica and Jean-Claude!

'Yucky! Yucky!' Dil exclaimed.

'That was easy!' Chuckie said.

'Way to go, Chuckie!' Tommy exclaimed.

'We knew you could do it!' Lil said.

Phil pumped the air with his fist. 'Let's get goin'!'

Chuckie scratched his head. He stared at all the buttons and levers. 'Gee, I wonder what this big one's for?'

He grabbed a switch and flipped it.

R-o-a-r!

Reptar sprang to life, sending the babies tumbling on to their behinds.

'Whoa!' they all cried at once.

Jean-Claude looked up from his paper, startled.

'Thank you for flying Air Angelica. Hope you

114

have a nice trip!' Angelica said, snickering. 'See you next fall!' Then she took off running.

Jean-Claude tossed down his newspaper and rose to his feet. 'You think you're so clever! But you're not as clever as Jean – '

He tried to take a step but he tripped over his tangled shoelaces and fell in a heap on the ground. 'Claugggghhhh!'

As Jean-Claude sprawled face-first on the floor, the huge mechanical Reptar stormed through the warehouse wall.

'Hey, you dumb babies!' Angelica shouted as she ran after them. 'Wait for me!'

'Uh, Tommy?' Lil said. 'We forgotted Angelica!'

'You say that like it's a bad thing,' Phil said.

'Chuckie, we gots to go back,' Tommy said.

'I don't know if I can, Tommy,' Chuckie replied. 'I barely know how to go forward.'

Angelica was running down a walkway at Reptar's head level. 'Wait for me!' she shouted. 'Do you know how hard it is to run in a flower girl dress?'

'Look! There's Angelica!' Lil cried.

'Stop the Reptar!' Angelica hollered. 'Ahhhhh!' She ran over a bridge across Reptar's path. Reptar walked under the bridge and emerged with Angelica hanging from his nose.

'Wow,' Lil said. 'Reptar's bogies look just like Angelica!'

An alarm on one of Reptar's control panels buzzed and flashed a warning, obstruction in the nose! An emergency control system sent a blast of compressed air out Reptar's nostrils, so that Reptar appeared to be sneezing Angelica into his hands in a cloud of soot.

'This is *not* the parade I wanted,' Angelica said.

Chapter 20

At Notre Dame Cathedral, Howard was video-taping everything.

He taped the singer as he sang a lovely wedding song from the balcony. He filmed the friends and family who waited quietly in their seats. He taped Chas and Stu standing next to the old priest at the altar.

Any minute now, Chas kept thinking, Coco and Chuckie and the children will get here and the wedding will begin. He rocked back and forth on his heels and tried not to whistle. Any day now . . .

Howard even taped Chas rocking back and forth on his squeaky shoes.

Chas sneaked a look at his watch.

Suddenly there was a noise at the back of church. Howard zoomed around with his video

117

camera and saw Coco LaBouche. She was racing down the aisle, yanking on the train of her long white dress. Her footsteps echoed off the high cathedral ceilings.

'Goodness! Here comes the bride!' Howard said.

Didi twisted around in her seat. 'Without the wedding march?' she exclaimed.

'Without the flower girl?' Drew asked.

'Without *Chuckie?*' Chas exclaimed.

Gasping for breath, Coco arrived at Chas's side. She smoothed down her skirt. Then she smiled at Chas as if it were the most ordinary thing in the world for a bride to charge down the aisle like an athlete in the hundred-metre dash. She turned back to the front and shook her fingers at the priest, as if shooing chickens along the road. 'Go! Go! Go!' she quickly told him. 'Start!'

Startled, the priest opened his mouth, unsure of how to begin.

But Chas interrupted. 'Coco, we can't start yet! Chuckie's not here. I want to share this moment with my son.'

'Oh, darling,' Coco said. She snaked her arms around his arm and fluttered her long dark lashes at him, 'we will tell him all about it. That's what video-tape is for.'

She turned to the priest. 'Go ahead,' she ordered him.

The confused priest wiped his forehead with his handkerchief. '*Bonjour*, everyone. I'd like to welcome the family and friends of Monsieur and Madame – '

'Yes, yes, they can read that in the programme,' Coco interrupted impatiently. 'Let's begin.' She smiled at Chas.

But Chas didn't smile back.

Something about her smile made his tummy feel funny.

⚜   ⚜   ⚜

I'm coming, Daddy! Chuckie thought as they stomped through Reptarland. Hold on!

'How do we get outta here?' Phil yelled.

'I think it's that way!' Chuckie hollered, and pointed. 'Or that way,' he said, changing again. 'No, that way!'

119

'As long as you're sure,' Lil said.

The people in Reptarland scrambled for cover – all except one. She waved. 'Hiya, Reptar!'

'It's Kimi!' Chuckie exclaimed. 'She looks like a bug from here!'

'Neat-o, let's pick her up,' Lil said.

Reptar's free claw uncoiled and scooped up Kimi. She squealed with delight. 'I didn't know you were a ride too!' she shouted.

Reptar crashed through the gates to the theme park and knocked the head off an animatronic character at the entrance. 'We hope you enjoyed Reptarland,' the head said, 'the happiest place on . . . on . . . on . . .' over and over, until another big robot came along and crushed it.

Robosnail!

'Going somewhere, my reptilian friend?' Robosnail said loudly. His voice sounded familiar. 'You babies cannot hide . . . from Jean-Claude, *Super Escargot!*'

Chuckie gasped and threw up his hands. The robotic Reptar copied Chuckie's movements

and threw Kimi and Angelica into its mouth.

'I'll have you babies for lunch – but not without the proper sauce!' Jean-Claude roared through Reptar's loudspeakers. His thumb punched a control button marked GOOEY and nozzles appeared on either side of the giant snail.

'Do you wanna pizza me, Sluggy? Wanna pizza me?' Kimi taunted, as she dangled from the edge of Reptar's mouth.

'Hey, can it, pineapple-head,' Angelica complained. A second later the gooey nozzles fired, slimed Reptar and the street, and forced the robot monster into a crazy dance.

'Stop wobbling, Chuckie,' Tommy complained, thinking it was just bad driving.

'Don't tell me,' Chuckie said, helpless. 'Tell my feet!' It was taking everything he had to keep Reptar standing up.

Reptar's huge feet thundered on the Paris streets, sending people running in every direction. He lunged past a park bench where a portrait artist was painting a happy couple . . . of dogs. It was Spike and Fifi! They barked,

121

sprang from the bench and bounded after the giant lizard.

Chuckie managed to steer Reptar up to the Arc de Triomphe. Then he slipped and shot under the legs of the big tower like a rugby player throwing himself over the line to score a try.

Jean-Claude ran Robosnail in after the lizard but slammed to a stop when his shell hit the sides of the Arc.

'Look, Chuckie,' Tommy said, pointing to a police blockade as they slid by. 'I think they want us to stop!'

'I do too!' Lil said.

'Stop in the name of France,' said a policeman through a bullhorn.

Chuckie was just about to regain Reptar's balance when the mechanical lizard's foot caught in the entrance to the underground Métro. Reptar stumbled over a police blockade and flipped, landing back-first on to a parked fire engine, which shot off like a skateboard. They were heading straight for the deep river that runs through the old city like ice-cold bathwater. The babies screamed.

122

Meanwhile, in another part of the city, Kira pedalled a bicycle as fast as she could in the direction of Notre Dame. She had no idea of all the excitement she was missing over at the Arc de Triomphe, where Reptar was speeding out of control.

Dil wasn't worried. He was in Reptar's control room, punching buttons with his rattle. It was by accident that he hit the parachute release that stopped Reptar from plunging into the river. The fire engine was not so lucky.

A hatch popped out of Reptar's mouth leading up to the top of Reptar's head. Lil peeked out. 'Hi, guys,' she said when she spotted Angelica and Kimi a couple of floors down in Reptar's jaws. Then she tossed a rope ladder over the side.

'Come on, you potty-heads!' Angelica hollered. 'We'll miss Mr Chuckie's Dad's wedding!'

'Where is it?, Kimi asked.

Phil stuck his head out of the hatch. 'We don't know. The growed-ups said something about a nutty dame.'

'Notre Dame!' Kimi said as she followed

123

Phil into the hatch. 'It's just past the Awful Tower!'

Angelica scrambled up the rope ladder behind Kimi until . . .

Crunch!

Something clamped on to Reptar's tail. It was Robosnail! He dragged Reptar off like a toy, babies and all. Angelica lost her grip on the ladder and clung tightly to one of Reptar's teeth.

Back at the church Chas still had that upset-tummy feeling, but he told himself it was only butterflies. Wedding day jitters. Or maybe it was because Coco was still trying to rush things. He was glad she was so eager to marry him. But he wanted everything to be perfect. He whispered something into the priest's ear.

The priest smiled and nodded. 'Charles would like to recite a poem to his bride.'

'It's our favourite, remember?' He smiled, then began to recite the poem they had shared on their first date in Reptarland. '"Dappled laughter – "'

'Touching,' Coco snapped. 'Now can we begin – '

'I'm not done yet!' Chas replied. 'But I'll hurry.'

Coco rolled her eyes. She wasn't sure she could bear to hear that corny poem again.

Reptar and Robosnail were locked in a fierce battle at the foot of the Eiffel Tower. The evil snail twirled Reptar around and around. Rivets popped off the lizard's tail. Inside Reptar the babies bounced around like beads in a baby's rattle. Luckily, Phil crash-landed against a rocket lever. A blast of fire roared out of Reptar's rear end and the beast shot up the tower like a space shuttle leaving the launchpad.

It didn't get far.

At the top of the tower, a wire cable snagged the monster's foot and stopped it dead. Angelica, on the other hand, kept going. She shot out of Reptar's jaws like a spitball.

'Look! Angelica's flying!' Tommy yelled.

Phil squinted. 'How'd she do that without a broom?'

It was a round trip – Angelica came right back. 'Ahhhhh!' she screamed, holding her pigtails like parachute cords.

'Ah . . . ah . . . ' Chuckie gasped, covering his face to sneeze. 'Choo!'

Chuckie was still wearing the control helmet. When he opened his hands to see what he had sneezed, Reptar copied and caught Angelica like a high-flying ball.

'It's . . . just Angelica,' Lil said.

Chuckie sneezed again. All the babies screamed as Reptar began to slide down the side of the Eiffel Tower as if he were sliding down a ladder.

Chapter 21

'Don't shoot!' the police shouted as they arrived at the tower. They'd spotted Angelica in Reptar's hand. 'It's got the girl!'

Reptar landed softly at the bottom of the tower. Then he turned and followed the movements of Chuckie's control helmet.

'Hang on, you guys,' Chuckie said. 'I think I gots a wedgie.' Chuckie wriggled the stuck nappy from his bottom. Reptar copied. Then off they went to Chas and Coco's wedding.

'Grasping fingers/dimpled chin . . .'

Over at Notre Dame, Chas was still reciting his poem. The poem he thought he *and* Coco loved. The poem Coco secretly hated.

'"Pudgy bellies, velvet skin . . ."'

Chas couldn't wait for his new life to begin.

Coco couldn't wait for the poem to end. 'Enough poetry! Marry us *now*!'

The priest began the vows. 'Do you, Charles, take Coco to be your lawfully wedded wife?'

Suddenly Chas's mouth went dry. His stomach flip-flopped. Nervously he swallowed. 'Uh, I – '

'He does and I do!' Coco cut in. 'Next?'

The battle between Robosnail and Reptar had moved to a bridge over the River Seine, near Notre Dame. Robosnail charged, smashing into Reptar's midsection. The lizard was losing.

'I'm sorry, Chuckie. It looks like you're going to end up with that mean lady for a mum,' Angelica said.

'Over my dad's potty,' Chuckie growled. 'Outta my way, slug-face!'

Determined, Chuckie began doing the same wild karate moves he had used in his dream. 'Chopkicky! Chopkicky! Take that! And that!'

Chuckie – through Reptar – hit, kicked and

bounced Robosnail around as if it were a little toy. The babies stared at Chuckie, stunned. 'All right, Chuckie!' they cheered.

Robosnail landed hard on the ground. Jean-Claude moaned.

'Another one bites the crust!' Angelica crowed.

'All right,' Chuckie cried, 'now let's get to that church!' But as he stepped over the slug, Jean-Claude made a desperate move with his screwdriver. He said, 'It's time for your one hundred-mile tune-up!' He was going to take Reptar apart piece by piece.

Then Phil leaned on the rocket lever one last time and – *wham!* – Robosnail was suddenly aflame, rocking back and forth on the bridge. 'I'm being sautéed,' Jean-Claude groaned. 'And I have no white wine!'

'Good job, Phil,' Chuckie said. 'Now let's go and save my daddy!'

⚜   ⚜   ⚜

Inside the church Chas and Coco were saying their vows.

'For better or worse,' the priest said.

'For better or worse,' Coco repeated. 'Next!'

The priest continued. 'For richer or – '

'Poorer!' Coco broke in. 'Sickness – '

'And in health?' the confused priest said.

'Must we repeat *everything*?' Coco asked.

The priest scratched his head and looked at his book. 'Oh, dear,' he said. 'I skipped a section.'

Boom! Reptar stomped towards the church.

Boom! Step . . . *Boom!* By step!

Notre Dame. It was a beautiful sight, except for the black shape in the river below it – the burned-out shell of Robosnail. From it Jean-Claude aimed a cannon loaded with a grappling hook. He planned to reel in Reptar like a harpooned whale.

'It's bathtime, babies,' Jean-Claude croaked from beneath a battered helmet as the remains of the giant snail rafted out from underneath the bridge. He pressed the steel trigger and fired the hook. It was a perfect shot. The hook locked on to Reptar's foot and tripped him

130

towards the river. It would have been a perfect victory for Jean-Claude if it hadn't been for Phil and Lil. Swinging from a control panel inside Reptar's head, they spotted the connectors that held Reptar's head on: two big rubber bands and a giant paper clip.

'Hey, look what I found!' Phil said.

'Papie clips and flubber bands!' Lil squealed.

Together the babies unfastened the rubber bands. Instantly Reptar's head rolled off its shoulders and landed on the bridge. Reptar's body dive-bombed on to Robosnail and flattened a limo parked in front of the church.

Jean-Claude and the limo driver got out just in time. An inflatable slide popped out of a side door in Reptar's head and Chuckie shot down it like a marble in a pinball chute!

'I'm coming, Daddy,' Chuckie cried.

'Go, Chuckie, go!' Tommy cheered.

Chapter 22

Chuckie raced up the steps of the church and stopped dead at the door.

Oh, no! A huge dragon-head door knob – just like the one on the princess's castle – glared down at him, guarding the way.

'I gots to be brave,' he said. He swallowed hard and pushed. Suddenly Spike charged up, followed by the poodle, and leaped towards Chuckie. The door swung open and all three of them tumbled inside.

Chuckie found himself looking at the backs of a lot of people's heads. He saw the priest standing at the front of the church.

And there! There's my daddy! And that mean lady!

'If anyone objects to this union,' the priest said, 'speak now or for ever hold your peace.'

'Noooooooooo!' Chuckie roared. 'No-No-No-Nooooooo!'

Everyone sprang to their feet and looked around as Chuckie ran down the aisle.

'Chuckie?' Chas exclaimed.

Sobbing, Chuckie reached his daddy and Chas scooped him up into his arms. 'Chuckie, Chuckie, it's okay, sweetheart. Daddy's here.'

Coco smoothed back her hair and smiled. 'So's his new mummy! Come here, little boy – '

Chas gave her a cold look. He had thought he loved her. He had thought she loved Chuckie. He had thought they could try to make a family. But he was wrong.

But Coco was used to getting what she wanted. She was not going to give up that easily. Not even when Jean-Claude came in, dripping wet, to announce, 'Madame, our kidnapping plot has failed.'

Coco glared at him a second and then flashed a charming smile at Chas. 'Ignore that *unemployed* fool!'

Chas frowned. 'Coco, the wedding is off,' he said. 'You are not the woman I thought you were.'

133

All the children entered the church with Spike and Fifi, who were dripping wet. Spike barked. All the grown-ups turned around and gasped.

'Hey, lady,' Angelica said. 'Looks like your plan to trick Mr Yummy-sushi didn't work after all.'

Coco's eyes bulged. Her teeth clenched like a vice. 'Pretty flower girls should be seen, not heard,' she warned.

From the back of the huge church came a soft but forceful voice. 'I would like to hear what the little one has to say.' Everyone stared at a silhouette in the doorway. It was a man wearing traditional Japanese clothes. Slowly he stepped into the light.

It was Mr Yamaguchi. Head of Reptarland. Coco's boss. He walked over to Angelica. Smiling warmly, he held out his hand to her.

Angelica took it. 'Okay,' she told the man. 'But lissen good, 'cuz I'm tired a' tellin' this story.' She cleared her throat and pointed at Coco. 'That cuckoo lady told her boss that she had a kid's heart in a jar, and she was gonna

134

marry Mr Chuckie's Daddy just so she could be president.'

'Listen, you traitorous, fork-tongued witch!' Coco muttered.

Mr Yamaguchi was outraged. 'Ms LaBouche!'

Coco's face switched to innocent surprise. 'Did I say fork-tongued?' Suddenly her face looked damp and her pulse showed in a big vein in her neck.

'You are dismissed,' Mr Yamaguchi curtly told her, then turned and left the church. Coco tried to follow, but the long train of her wedding gown was pinned to the floor under the weight of several babies.

'Dismissed? But no one fires Coco LaBouche! Coco LaBouche fires others! Coco LaBouche *is* Reptarland!'

Then she turned to the babies. 'Off the gown, you revolting carpet mice!' she growled.

'Lissen, lady,' Angelica said. 'Nobody messes with my dumb babies 'cept *me*!'

Coco stuck out her tongue. Then she turned with a defiant *harumph!*

135

Ri-i-i-i-i-i-i-p!

The entire back of her dress ripped off.

Jean-Claude couldn't resist. 'I see London, I see France. I see Coco's underpants!'

Then Coco shrieked and stormed out of the church. Everyone fell silent and looked at one another. No one was quite sure what to do.

No one except Chas Finster, who gazed down the long aisle at a figure in the doorway. Everyone turned to see who it was.

It was Kira. Her long journey from Coco's car to the church was over. With her was Kimi. Together they joined Chas and Chuckie at the front of the church. 'Chuckie, I have something that belongs to you,' Kira said. She reached into her bag and pulled out Chuckie's teddy bear. His Wawa. With a big smile, Chuckie held out his arms and hugged Wawa tight.

Kira sighed. That was the easy part. She turned to Chas. Time for the hard part.

'Chas,' Kira began, 'I'm so sorry. I wanted to tell you about Coco, but – '

'No, no, no. It's my fault, Kira. I guess I got caught up in the romance of Paris.' Chas gazed

at Chuckie fondly. 'I'm sorry, little guy. '"Oh, how my heart beats wild . . ."'

Kira joined him in reciting the next line. '"Each time I hold my precious child."'

Chas looked surprised and said, 'Wait – you know that poem?'

Kira nodded and replied, 'It's *my* favourite!'

He looked at Chuckie in his arms. Chuckie was smiling at Kira as if she were a princess. Or better yet, as if she were the most wonderful mummy in the world.

Six months later Chuckie felt like the happiest boy in the world. Not only that. He had the happiest dad in the world too.

A gong chimed – the sound of good fortune. Chas and Kira smiled at each other as they stood in a large banquet hall, surrounded by family and friends. They had just got married! And they were just about to cut the wedding cake.

In a darkened meeting room off the main hall, the Bobfather sat comfortably in a leather

chair. Kimi stood dutifully by his side. The Bobfather was stroking Wawa.

'No fair, Bobfather,' Angelica said. 'We've been back home for a bunch of yesterdays, and you still haven't delivered the goods. I got you a new mummy. Now where's my fashion show?'

Kimi glared. 'Angelica, you show him no 'aspect! You can't talk to him like . . .'

Chuckie, the Bobfather, raised his hand. 'Angelica, you come to me on the day of my daddy's weddin' to ask me for Cynthia châteaus, and pony staples, and jewley tiaras, and a bunch a stuff I can't *never* get you!'

Suddenly Susie Carmichael burst in. 'There you are, you guys! Come on!' she said. 'The growed-ups are giving away all the cake!'

'Outta my way, droolies!' Angelica cried, and pushed her way out of the door.

Chuckie got down from the chair. Then he placed his bear on it, fixed his bow and gave him a pat.

'Wawa's a really nice bear,' Kimi said.

'Thanks. My old mummy gived him to me,' Chuckie said.

138

'Do you ever miss her?' Kimi asked.

'Sometimes,' Chuckie told her. 'But then I 'member she's up there watching me from heaven.'

Chas and Kira came in and found them. 'There's my little guy,' Chas said. He tousled Chuckie's hair. Then he turned to Kimi. 'Kimi, sweetheart? May I have this dance?'

And Kira said, 'Chuckie? Would you like to dance with your new mummy?'

As Chuckie and Kira swirled on to the dance floor, Grandpa Lou opened a box of confetti. Chuckie gazed up at his new mum and saw colourful sparkles raining down.

Magic.

Out in the main hall, Angelica headed for the last piece of cake. It had an enormous icing rose.

'Cynthia, that last piece has our names bitten all over it.'

She reached for it, when . . .

'Angelica! You fibbed to me!'

139

'Huh?' Angelica spun around. Susie Carmichael stared at her, hands on her hips.

'You didn't have a fashion show in Paris! Tommy told me!'

Angelica fumed. 'Tommy wouldn't know fashion if it plopped him on that bald head!'

'Well, at least Tommy wouldn't tell lies, Angelica!' Susie said, and walked off.

Angelica stuck out her tongue and turned back towards the cake. But it was too late.

The other babies were just finishing it off.

'You're right, Philip,' said Lil around a mouthful of icing. The bride and groom figures from the top of the cake were in her hand. 'The feets do taste better than the head.'

'Who do you babies think you are?' Angelica demanded.

Tommy shrugged. 'Well, I'm Tommy and this is Lil . . .'

Phil snorted. 'And she calls *us* dumb!'

'Give me that cake right now!' Angelica shrieked. A big, sloppy glob splatted on her face.

'Good throw, Dilly,' Tommy said.

'Yucky!' Dil squealed happily.

Angelica wiped a glob of icing off and aimed for Dil. 'That's it, drooly! Prepare to meet your caker!' Then she threw the icing and hit Tommy on the head.

'Hey, guys,' Chuckie said. 'Whatcha doin?'

Tommy fired a wad of icing at Angelica but missed, and got Chuckie instead.

'Oh!' Chuckie exclaimed. 'A food fight!'

And then cake and icing were flying everywhere.

Phil threw the groom figurine and it bounced off Angelica's head. 'DeVille,' she screamed, 'when I get my hands on you, you'll be wishin' you were sleepin' with the goldfishies!' And she took off after him.

'Come on, you guys,' Kimi said. 'Phil needs our help!'

'But Kimi,' Chuckie argued, 'Angelica's biggerer and meaner!'

It didn't matter. Kimi was already running after Angelica.

'Well, Tommy,' Chuckie said, 'I guess this is how it's gonna be from now on.'

Chuckie and Tommy both laughed.

About the Authors

Cathy East Dubowski and Mark Dubowski started writing and illustrating children's books while they lived in a small apartment in New York City. Now they work in two old barns on Morgan Creek near Chapel Hill, North Carolina. They live with their daughters, Lauren and Megan, and their two golden retrievers, Macdougal and Morgan. They also wrote the novelization of the first Rugrats feature film, *The Rugrats Movie*; as well as many other Rugrats books.

©2000 Paramount Pictures and Viacom International Inc. All rights reserved. NICKELODEON, *Rugrats*, and all related titles, logos, and characters are trademarks of Viacom International Inc. *Rugrats* created by Arlene Klasky, Gabor Csupo, and Paul Germain.